Inside the Mind of a Criminal . . .

I was sitting in the back of a police cruiser. Me. Frank Hardy. Son of Fenton Hardy, a former cop. It was just so wrong. In so many ways.

Wait. No. It's not me, Frank Hardy, getting a police escort from the airport to Camp Wilderness, I reminded myself. *It's Steve Neemy.*

But the weird thing was—I still felt kind of ashamed. I felt like everyone in the little town of Greenville was looking at me. Wondering what Frank Hardy had done to get himself sent to reform camp.

I told myself to start thinking like Steve. Steve was supposed to be a hard case. A guy with attitude. A guy who had no use for Linc Saunders and his rehabilitation program.

THE HARDY BOYS

UNDERCOVER BROTHERS™

Available from Simon & Schuster

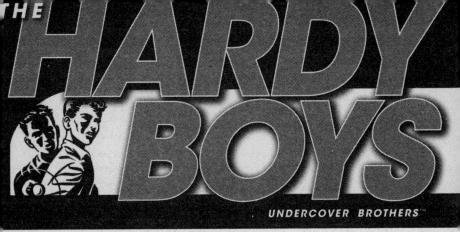

THE HARDY BOYS

UNDERCOVER BROTHERS™

#7 Operation: Survival

FRANKLIN W. DIXON

Aladdin Paperbacks
New York   London   Toronto   Sydney

❧ALADDIN PAPERBACKS
An imprint of Simon & Schuster
Children's Publishing Division
1230 Avenue of the Americas
New York, NY 10020

Copyright © 2005 by Simon & Schuster, Inc.

THE HARDY BOYS MYSTERY STORIES and HARDY BOYS
UNDERCOVER BROTHERS are a trademarks of Simon & Schuster, Inc.
ALADDIN PAPERBACKS and colophon are trademarks of
Simon & Schuster, Inc.
Designed by Lisa Vega
The text of this book was set in Aldine 401BT.
Manufactured in the United States of America
First Aladdin Paperbacks edition December 2005
10 9 8 7

Library of Congress Control Number: 2005930514
ISBN-13: 978-1-4169-0067-2
ISBN-10: 1-4169-0067-5

TABLE OF CONTENTS

Operation: Survival

1.

DOUBLE BLACK DIAMOND

"All those weenies are lined up waiting for us to hit a trough and eat snow."

The Bear Mountain skiers are tough. They love to hang around the Outer Limits trail. You crash and burn—make that crash and *freeze*—and they laugh. And clap. It's what they do for fun when they aren't skiing themselves.

And here my brother and I were, about to join the show. I hoped it would be a show that made people *oooh* and *ahhh*. Not *ha, ha, ha*.

"You worried?" Frank asked as we swung ourselves onto the ski lift. He waved to the people lined up with their stupid hot chocolates and their stupid smiles.

1

I snorted, as if I didn't want to waste words answering such a wet-butt question. Except I was worried. Not much. A little. I'm talking teeny. Outer Limits is ranked double black diamond. That means a trail of extreme extremeness. I'd skied black diamond before. Never a DB.

How much harder can it be? I asked myself.

The ski lift went up. I glanced down. *Yowch!* A guy in a red jacket hit a mogul in a not-good way. Can I offer some advice? If you're a bad skier, don't wear red. It makes you way too easy to see from the lift. And after the seeing comes the finger-pointing and the snickering.

"It's her. She's going for the package," Frank told me.

I pulled my eyes away from the red jacket and looked at the blond woman riding the chair in front of us. Yep. She'd just snatched the envelope of blackmail cash from under her seat. Now it was stowed in her little backpack.

She wouldn't have the money for long. Frank and I were going to get it back. Which would make a lot of kids at Markham High very happy.

They had trusted Blondie Blackmailer. They'd made friends with her when she pretended to be just another new student at their school. Really good friends. They'd thought she was the kind of friend you could tell all your most embarrassing secrets.

How could they know she made a career of enrolling in high schools in rich neighborhoods, sucking up all the dirt like our Aunt Trudy's trusty Hoover, and then demanding piles of dough to keep quiet?

They couldn't. No one expects something like that.

I was glad Frank and I were going to be bringing her down. She was an especially scummy scumbag, in my opinion.

Blondie dismounted from her chair. Frank and I were right behind her. My breath felt like it started going the wrong way when I rounded the first bend.

I knew the run was *steep*. But from up here, looking down, it was *steep*. I'm talkin' ste-e-e-e-e-p. Twelve hundred feet of vertical in a half mile.

After the bend you could go right—and cross under the ski lift. Or you could go left—a narrower path. Blondie went left.

My twin tips slapped the ground like I was trying to do a drum solo on the snow as Frank and I chased after her. At least I stayed on the skis. And on the Outer Limits, that's saying something.

I had to give her props—she could ski. She

3

could wear any color jacket she wanted, with no fear of the snickering and fingerpointing.

Frank was moving up on her. I spotted a deep rut line and rode that hard, my teeth slamming together the whole way. I was neck and neck with Frank now.

Blondie shot a look over her shoulder. Snow was splashed across her goggles. But I could see her green eyes widen. She was surprised to see us on her tail. Surprised and *not* happy.

Our blackmailing friend took us over another mogul. A mogul that would be the mountain anywhere else. Then she led us right toward a trench. She swerved at the last second and managed to avoid it.

But Frank and I didn't end up having that option. We plunged straight down into it—and up the other side.

You didn't gain much with that maneuver, Blondie, I thought. My skis jittered over the crisscrossing tracks in the snow. I leaned forward, so far I thought I was going to face-plant. But the maneuver gained me some speed. I pulled up alongside the blackmailer.

Frank made his move a second later. He started to slide into position on Blondie's other side.

Then she did something totally unexpected.

4

Make that totally insane. She whipped her body toward the tree line. And powered off the trail and right into the woods.

I heard Frank give a cry of surprise. But he didn't hesitate. He rocketed off the trail. I was right behind him—and soon found myself on a nightmare natural slalom. No flimsy little flags here. Just lots of pine trees. Running into one of them wouldn't tickle.

I swung to the left. To the right. To the left. A branch slapped against my goggles. Another one cut across my cheek. I'd had about enough of this. Forget skiing. It was football time.

Arrghh! I let out a growl and pointed myself at Blondie. She was just past a nice-sized snow bump. I took it. Tried to get as much lift as I could. When I came down, I brought her with me.

Tackle! Can I get a cheer from the cheerleaders in the short skirts?

I ate snow as I hit the ground. Snow and a little blood from that cut on my face. Electric snowflakes bounced around in front of my eyes.

When I managed to sit up, I saw that Frank had Blondie's backpack in his hands.

I reached over and snapped one of the blackmailer's bindings loose. Then I yanked the ski free. Just as a safety precaution.

Blondie was an amazing athlete. But even she couldn't get far on one stick.

"Give me that backpack!" Blondie ordered Frank. I tried to remember if I'd ever heard a girl sound so furious with my brother. Girls usually get all lovey-dovey oooey-gooey around him. Even though I'm the cute one.

"Sure. It's yours." Frank tossed Blondie Blackmailer the pack—but he held on to the cash he'd removed. He waved the envelope of money at her. "This isn't."

"Hey, do you think anybody would mind if the two of us snagged a couple of bucks before we return that?" I asked my brother. "I've gotta buy one of those T-shirts that say 'I Survived the Outer Limits.'"

Frank frowned at me.

My brother can never tell when I'm kidding.

"Don't worry," I told him. "I know we're the good guys."

2.

MURDER?

"Girls don't like good guys," Chet Morton complained. "They like bad boys. That's my problem."

I tried not to smile. But it was a little hard. I thought our friend Chet was totally wrong about his lack of success with girls.

It wasn't that he wasn't a bad-boy type. It was that he pretty much never attempted to talk to a girl of any kind.

Not that I don't understand that. I have a little girl phobia myself. I start blushing when I talk to them. And I hate to blush. So I don't talk to them much.

"You're totally right," Joe told Chet. "And it's totally unfair. Why should Belinda Conrad drool

7

over Frank all the time just because Frank's totally e-e-e-e-evil? She should have more appreciation for the good guys like you and me."

Chet blew a straw wrapper at Joe. "He's mocking me. Do you see that, Frank? Your brother sees my pain. And he mocks."

"It's just that your particular kind of pain is so mockable," Joe answered.

I completely ignored Joe. And kind of ignored Chet. I'd just gotten to an interesting part in my bio textbook. It was all about how eye color is determined by three genes, not just two. Blue-eyed parents can actually have a child with brown eyes, and—

JOE

Joe here. I love the wonderful world of science as much as the next guy. I do. Science has given us many wonderful things. The polio vaccine. Bubble-gum tape. But I don't think you really want to hear all this biology blabber right now. Am I right?

Frank here. This is my part of the story. So as I was saying, I was reading up on genetics, half listening to my brother make dumb jokes and our friend Chet complain about his lack of a love life. Then Vijay Patel showed up in the caf with a pizza in one of those red pizza-warmer bags. He headed right over to our table and put the pie in front of me.

"You ordered pizza?" Chet burst out. "You can't order pizza here." He turned to Joe. "Can you?"

"The principal ordered it for him," Vijay explained. "Some new thing where every month the top student gets a pizza for lunch. My boss is donating. One topping only. No soda."

Patel's lying skills are impressive, I thought. I knew his boss hadn't made any donation to the school. Patel didn't even really work at a pizza place. Pizza delivery guy is just a cover for him. He's ATAC, like me and Joe. That's American Teens Against Crime. It's an organization our dad created.

See, sometimes there's a situation where the police need someone on the inside. Someone under twenty. That's where Joe, Vijay, and I—and the rest of the ATAC team—come in.

Vijay hasn't gotten the chance to do big-time

undercover work yet. His job is coordinating the missions with the police. But he's always trying to get a field assignment. And with his lying skills, I think he'd be excellent. I made a mental note to talk to Dad about that.

"Enjoy, bestest boy in school." Vijay gave a half salute along with a half smirk, then walked away.

My heartbeat accelerated a little. Joe and I were about to get our next assignment. That never stops feeling exciting.

"I need to hit the bathroom," I told Joe.

Joe immediately stood up. "Me too." He grabbed the pizza box.

"You're takin' the pizza?" Chet complained.

"Sometimes there's a line for the bathroom," Joe answered. "And waiting makes me hungry."

It was a dumb-sounding excuse. But Joe and I couldn't open that box in front of Chet. There was info on our mission in there. And ATAC is top secret. Even from friends like Chet. Even from our mom. And our mom is exceptionally cool for a mother. Even for a person.

Joe led the way to the bad bathroom—the one with one broken toilet and two faucets that always manage to spray water on the front of your pants. It was empty as usual. I reached over and opened the pizza box.

I grabbed the foil-wrapped package on top of the pie. Joe grabbed a slice of pepperoni. "Game player," I instructed.

Joe finished the slice in two bites. He pulled his portable video-game player out of his backpack. Ever since we were inducted into ATAC, we'd taken to carrying it with us. I had another player in my room.

I unwrapped the package. "Operation: Survival," I read off the front of the game cartridge.

Well, it looked like a DVD, or CD. That's the format our mission assignments come in. Part of the top-secret thing. And the disc actually changes into a normal CD after we watch it. Impressive technology.

"Sounds like a fun one." Joe snapped the "game" into place.

A montage started up, backed by some rock-infused country music. Two guys rappelling down the side of a mountain. A bunch of guys white-water rafting. A canoe race. Then a wooden sign at the head of a dirt road leading into a forest: WELCOME TO CAMP WILDERNESS.

"Looks like ATAC is sending us on vacation. Maybe it's a reward for the kick-butt job we did last time."

The image on the little screen changed again—to

a group of guys sitting around a campfire. Then to a close-up of one of the guys' faces. He sort of reminded me of Chet.

Chet usually looks like he's about to laugh. Which is because Chet thinks almost everything is funny. Well, except the state of his love life.

Anyway, this guy had that kind of look too.

The color shot of the guy morphed into a black-and-white police photo. The music faded out. "Whoa," Joe muttered.

Exactly. The guy didn't look like he was about to laugh anymore. He looked dead.

Text began to scroll across the screen. Part of the article that went with the photo, I figured.

"Zack Maguire was sent to Camp Wilderness in the Moosehead Lake region of Maine. The camp is an experimental program to rehabilitate teens who have been convicted of crimes," I read. "Maguire was two weeks from completing his sentence at the camp when he recently fell to his death while mountain climbing."

Zack's photo was still in the upper right-hand corner of the screen. Now I took in the fact that one of his legs was bent at an angle that no leg should be able to go. His fall from the side of a mountain explained that.

The text kept flowing across the screen. I had to

read quickly not to miss anything. "'Zack should never have been sentenced to the camp,' Maguire's mother claimed. "'He'd never spent any time in the outdoors. He wasn't used to hiking and climbing or camping.'"

The article went on. "Strenuous physical challenges such as the mountain-climbing expedition are a large part of Camp Wilderness's program. The director of the camp, Linc Saunders, believes that the challenges give the teens a sense of accomplishment and self-worth, and that these positive feelings lead to rehabilitation."

The photo of Zack was replaced by one of Linc Saunders. He looked kind of like a lumberjack in a cartoon.

Big. The guy was big. Big arms. Even big teeth. And hair everywhere. Full beard. Chest hair curling out of his black and red plaid shirt.

"'I deeply regret what happened to Zack Maguire under my watch,' Saunders said at a press conference. 'But I hope that the death of one boy will not discredit all we've accomplished at Camp Wilderness. Ninety-nine percent of the teens who participate in my program haven't committed another crime. They are out in the world, making real contributions to society. And they were willing to push themselves during the program. They weren't afraid to work hard. And they found their core of steel.'"

"That's kinda cold." Joe flicked Saunders's face with his finger.

I agreed. Saunders coughed up one sentence about Zack's death. Then he started talking about how great his camp was. And how all the kids turned into model citizens. It was like he didn't give a monkey's butt about Zack.

The color of the text turned from black to bright red. "'Saunders briefly ran a similar camp in Montana—Camp Character,'" I read. "'The camp was quietly closed down after a teenage girl, Samantha Previn, died there while white-water rafting.'"

"I'm seeing a pattern here. Not a happy pattern," Joe commented.

"Yeah, I don't think ATAC is sending us on a fun-filled vacation after all," I said.

I continued reading. "'I'm not surprised another kid ended up dead under Linc's supervision,' a worker from the Montana camp, who would only speak anonymously, commented. 'Linc would rather kill a kid than damage his success rate. The white-water accident that closed down Camp Character was no accident. Linc's methods weren't working on the kid, so the kid ended up dead. You don't screw up the statistics when you're dead.'"

14

The picture of the kids around the campfire returned. It was hard to look at Zack's grinning face, now that I knew what had happened to him. Now that I knew he hadn't made it out of the camp alive.

"Your mission is to go undercover at Camp Wilderness." The voice coming out of the game player was clearly electronically generated. There was no way to identify the speaker, but we knew it was Q.T.

"You must determine if Zack Maguire's death was accidental. Or if he was murdered."

3.
COVER STORIES

"We need you to sign permission slips for a science trip," I said that night at dinner.

My parents, Frank, and Aunt Trudy all stared at me. Probably because what they heard was more like "Wah neeg oo oo gine ermissgin ips or ience rip."

Or maybe because they were all horrified by the sight of me talking with my mouth way too full.

I couldn't help it. When Aunt Trudy serves up her chocolate chip cookie pie, my mouth is going to be full. It's a cookie. And a pie. That should explain everything. Unless your taste buds have been surgically removed.

I chugged down some moo juice—as I used to

call milk when I was four—and tried again. "Permission slips. We need you to sign them. The top kids in all the science classes get to spend a week at Moosetail Lake."

"Moose*head*," Frank corrected.

Tail. Head. What was the big deal? They were both attached to the moose. I don't know why Frank has to be so technical about stuff.

"It's in Maine," I said. "We're going to study the ecosystem of the lake."

Did you like how I tossed in the word ecosystem? I did that for Mom. She's really into recycling and saving the planet and everything. I figured if she was leaning toward saying no, using the *E* word might push her toward yes.

"Studying the ecosystem." Mom shot a smile at me. "While canoeing, and rafting, and—"

I held up both hands. "Okay, you got me." *Like always,* I thought. Sometimes when I'm around Mom, I feel like my skull is made of cling wrap. Every thought visible.

"There will be some fun to be had," I confessed. "But I'm sure we'll learn something, too. So, will you sign?" I slid the phony permission slips across the table.

We got the slips in our ATAC pizza package—

17

along with two plane tickets to Maine, details about our false identities, and bios of Zack Maguire and Linc Saunders.

Mom and Dad exchanged a glance. You know, one of those glances that are like entire conversations. "I guess we can survive without you two for a week." Mom pulled a pen from behind her ear. She always has a pen stuck back there. I think it's a research librarian thing. She signed and gave me back the slips.

Aunt Trudy took the pen from Mom and started jotting down a list on the back of a grocery receipt she found in her pocket. "Underwear—ten pairs each. Socks—twelve pairs each. Sweaters, wool—," she mumbled.

"Aunt T, we're only going for a week," I reminded her.

"And you're telling me in that week one of you isn't going to fall into the lake at least once and need a complete change of clothing?" Aunt Trudy continued writing.

Aunt T thinks Frank and I are about five. I mean, come on, who falls into a lake? I haven't fallen into a body of water since I was . . . okay, since I was thirteen. But usually I have no problem surviving on one pair of underwear a day.

Honestly, I can survive on less. I don't really

understand the need for new underwear every single day. Every couple works for me.

Mom had more important things on her mind than wet boxers. "At this time of year, you may run into some black bears up there," she told me and Frank. "If you see one, do what the Native Americans used to."

She lifted her arms into the air. Still holding her fork. She didn't realize she was in danger of ending up with some meatloaf on her head.

"Hold your hands over your head and say, 'Hello, Brother Bear. I did not mean to disturb you. I will leave your territory and leave you in peace,'" Mom instructed.

"What about that bear spray? One of the jumbo cans. I'm thinkin' that might be a better way to deal with Brother Bear," I said.

They really do make the stuff. I thought it was a joke the first time I saw an ad for it in a camping magazine. Because once you're close enough to a bear to zap it with spray, you're already a lot closer than I want to be. But I have to say, the spray seemed a lot safer to me than Mom's method.

"The spray might just make them angry," Dad jumped in. "And an angry bear is nothing you want to deal with."

"A lot of bears attack simply because they're

surprised," Mom explained. "That's why talking to them is good. You don't have to use the exact words I gave you—say anything. You can even sing if you want to—"

"Mom, what are you saying? We've all heard Frank sing in the shower. It's enough to make a baby kitten go on a killing spree."

Mom shook her head at me. But she smiled, too. So the head shake didn't really count. "Just make noise and keep your hands over your head. That makes you look bigger."

"If they do attack, you're supposed to play dead, right?" Frank asked.

"Good thing I just helped a kid do research on bears. I know all the answers," Mom replied. "You should play dead—even if the bear bites you. Except with black bears. Black bears are scavengers, not hunters. So if one bites, it's probably decided you're food. That means you have to go on the attack."

I nodded. Good to know. But I had the feeling Frank and I should be a lot more worried about Linc Saunders—a potential murderer—than bears.

Frank reached for the last piece of cookie pie. But I got there first. "I'm gonna take this upstairs. I need to get some homework in," I announced.

"Me too," Frank said. I led the way up to my room.

"Wimps, wimps, wimps," Playback called.

"It's not nice to talk to Frank that way," I told our parrot.

Playback ruffled his feathers. Frank ignored me. He does that a lot. He flopped down on my bed. I pulled the files we'd received from ATAC out of the top drawer of my desk.

There was a file for Brian Moya. And a file for Steve Neemy. Neemy's stats included dark brown hair and brown eyes, so I handed that file over to Frank.

I flipped open the file for Brian Moya. The blond hair, blue eyes description matched me. "Brian Moya, Brian Moya, Brian Moya," I said aloud. I wanted to get a feel for the name.

"You sound like Playback," Frank commented.

This time *I* ignored *him*. "Brian Moya," I said one more time. Then I started to read the police report for Brian. Make that me. "Wow. I was arrested for shoplifting three times," I told Frank. "The last time, the judge ordered me to a stay at Camp Wilderness."

"I trashed a convenience store in an act of gang violence," Frank answered.

I tried to imagine Frank trashing anything. It made my head hurt. He doesn't even trash his bedroom. He's freakishly neat. I've been thinking

21

about having him studied by a team of scientists. I suspect he isn't a hundred percent human.

"Okay, so we should flesh out our cover stories." Frank stared up at the ceiling. "Steve Neemy is from Brooklyn. So what gang should I have been in?"

I sat down in front of my computer and Googled "Brooklyn" and "gang." A lot of Mafia stuff came up. Not what I was looking for.

I tried "teen gang." Yeah, this is more what we needed. "There's some stuff on big gangs, like the Vice Lords and the Gangster Disciples. But if a guy from one of those gangs is at the camp—"

"It would be way too easy for them to figure out I'm a fake," Frank finished for me. We do that sometimes. Complete each other's thoughts.

"Right. Even if you studied from now until we leave, you'd never be able to get down all the details," I agreed. Which is saying something. Because Frank's a study champion.

"So Steve Neemy—"

"You mean you," I interrupted.

"Right. So I'm not from a major league gang. I'm from a smaller league gang," Frank said. "Just me and some guys from the neighborhood. And I'm not one of the leaders or anything. I'm—"

A knock cut Frank off. "Enter!" I called.

22

Dad came inside and closed the door behind him. "Your mother is doing a bear-by-bear survival breakdown for you two. I think I convinced her she didn't have to include polar bears. You know your mom. Thorough. Plus, she worries."

Like Dad doesn't. He worries a lot more than Mom does. But maybe that's because he knows we're ATAC. That gives him extra stuff to be worried about.

"You all ready for the trip?" Dad asked.

Let me translate the fatherspeak: *Are you sure you don't need my expert advice? Since I am an only partly retired PI, and I was a cop for a million years, and, oh, yeah, I founded ATAC?*

Frank and I keep waiting for Dad to realize we can handle ourselves. We've completed tons of missions.

"Yep. We're just doing a little prep on our cover stories," Frank said.

Dad leaned against the doorframe. Like he was just casually hanging out. But I could see how tight the muscles in his neck were. "Uh-huh. And that's going okay?" he asked.

Translation: *I have years, and years, and yes, years more experience than you boys. I think it would be smart of you to ask for a little advice.*

"Going great," I answered. I did that thing

23

where you mean to nod once, but then end up looking like one of those bobblehead dolls. I hoped all those extra head bobs would convince Dad that I really meant everything was going great. That he didn't really have to worry, because Frank and I were on top of things.

Then there was one of those silences. You know the kind. A silence that is basically a battle of wills. Who will speak first? Who's gonna crack?

Frank didn't talk. I didn't talk. Dad didn't talk. Even Playback didn't talk—for once.

I wanted to throw Dad a bone. I did. Just give him my opinion on the Linc Saunders is-he-a-murderer-or-not question. Or ask him his opinion.

But the thing is, parents are hard to train. If Frank and I let Dad talk the case over with us this time, he'd want to do it every time.

And Dad always has these retro ideas about everything. For example, he doesn't see why we need our ultimate, extreme motorcycles. I mean, he makes sure we've got everything we need—he totally souped them up a short while ago—but he'd rather have us ride Vespas or something. Again, because he worries.

And probably because he didn't get to ride an awesome motorcycle back in the day, so he doesn't see any reason we should now.

"Well, if you need me, you know where I'll be," Dad finally said.

Hey, we won. But we don't always. Dad is truly superior at the silence game.

Words came pouring out of me the second the door closed behind him. "So you're going to be from a farm team kinda gang. Nothing that anybody but you and your crime-lovin' buds know about. Do you have a name? The Pythons? The Vicious Sisters? The Polar Bears?"

"Let's get back to that," Frank said. "I thought of something while—" He hesitated.

"While we were waiting for Dad to realize we're big boys who can handle our missions on our own?" I asked.

"Yeah. Anyway, I think that one of us should pretend to be unathletic," Frank went on. "I have the feeling that Saunders won't have any patience for a guy who can't meet all those physical challenges he lines up."

"I can see that. That quote from him made it sound like he didn't have a lot of respect for kids who weren't able to find their core of heavy metal."

"Steel," Frank corrected me.

Will he ever get my sense of humor?

"And Zack's mother said Zack didn't have any

experience camping or anything like that," I added. "Maybe he kept messing up. Maybe Zack wasn't strong enough to be the kind of Camp Wilderness success story Saunders loves."

"Maybe," Frank agreed. "I think it would be interesting to see how Saunders treats someone who isn't in great shape."

"Well, you're going to have to be that someone. I'm a genius at the undercover stuff. But no one's going to believe I'm a couch potato." I flexed for Frank. "Maybe I should be a guy with attitude. A guy who isn't going to become a rehabilitation poster child for Saunders, no matter what. I think that would bug him as much as an out-of-shape kid."

"One of us should definitely give Saunders some attitude," Frank said. "That's a great idea."

"So you be the wimp, wimp, wimp. And I'll be the outlaw who won't be brought down by a stay at Saunders's pathetic little camp."

Frank pulled a quarter out of his pocket. "I'll flip you for it."

"Do you really think you can pull off an extreme bad-boy attitude? You're not exactly . . . Let's face it, Frank. You're a teacher's pet kinda guy. Every adult you've ever met loves you."

Frank gave me the Look of Doom. "Heads," I said.

The quarter went up. And came back down—
tail up.

"And you lose. Shall I call you Mr. Potato, or do
you prefer Spuddy?" Frank asked.

I shrugged. "At least I'll be able to check out
Chet's theory."

"What?"

"So I have to pretend to be out of shape and
everything. But I'm still Brian Moya, shoplifter.
And that means I'm still a Bad Boy. With capital Bs.
If Chet's right, the girls at the camp should think
I'm The Man."

4.

WELCOME TO CAMP WILDERNESS

I was sitting in the back of a police cruiser. Me. Frank Hardy. Son of Fenton Hardy, a former cop. It was just so wrong. In so many ways.

Wait. No. It's not me, Frank Hardy, getting a police escort from the airport to Camp Wilderness, I reminded myself. *It's Steve Neemy.*

But the weird thing was—I still felt kind of ashamed. I felt like everyone in the little town of Greenville was looking at me. Wondering what Frank Hardy had done to get himself sent to reform camp.

I told myself to start thinking like Steve. Steve was supposed to be a hard case. A guy with attitude. A guy who had no use for Linc Saunders and his rehabilitation program.

I met the gaze of the middle-aged man who was using the crosswalk while the cruiser was stopped at a red light.

What are you looking at? I tried to ask him with my eyes. *What have you done with your life that's so special? What gives you the right to feel superior to me?*

The man looked away first. Good. I'd channeled Steve pretty well.

The cruiser exited the main street of the town. It was only a couple of blocks long. A little grocery. A bakery. A bait shop where you could get a hunting and fishing license. That kind of thing.

The houses started coming farther and farther apart. Then we turned onto a dirt road. About five miles down it, I saw the sign. The sign that we'd seen in our mission assignment: WELCOME TO CAMP WILDERNESS.

Looking at it made all the little hairs on my arms and the back of my neck stand on end.

"This is it, huh?" Joe said.

The cop behind the wheel glanced over his shoulder. "This is it," he answered. "Last chance. You screw up here, and it's straight to juvie. Do not pass Go. Do not collect two hundred dollars."

He didn't say it in a nasty kind of way. More in an FYI kind of way. Or even an I-don't-want-to-see-you-mess-your-life-up way.

"Unless you happen to turn eighteen while you're at the camp," his partner added. He gave us a not-all-that-friendly smile, and I noticed he had a gap between his front teeth. "Then you go straight to big-boy prison if you don't keep your nose clean here."

We pulled up in front of a small, plain building made of pine planks. A couple of jeeps were parked in front of it. A quarter mile or so behind it was a long row of bunks.

"Somehow I don't think we're going to be getting little mints on our pillows," Joe said.

I ignored him. But not in the way I usually do. I did it in a Steve Neemy why-are-you-even-talking-to-me way.

The cops opened the back doors for me and Joe. We couldn't open them ourselves. The backseats of cop cars don't have door handles on the inside. Which is logical. Can't give the criminal types an easy escape route.

Then the cops marched us into what turned out to be Linc Saunders's place. An office, bedroom, kitchenette combo. "Neemy and Moya for you," the gap-toothed cop announced.

Saunders nodded and the cops left. "Have a seat, boys. I was just about to run through the Camp

Wilderness philosophy for Miss Hanks here. She's a new arrival as well."

The teenage girl sitting on the sofa in front of Saunders's desk didn't look over at me and Joe. She kept her eyes on the bearskin rug on the floor. I tried to keep my eyes off it.

See, my grandmother used to have this fox scarf kind of thing. It had its head still attached—just like the bear rug did. When I was little I used to dream that the fox came alive and tried to claw my face—

You know what? This is not information you need to know. Back to the story.

I sat down on one side of the girl. Joe planted himself on the other.

The girl was cute, I'll admit it. I wondered if Joe was thinking about Chet's bad-boy theory.

Saunders leaned back in his leather chair. The front legs came off the ground. The back legs creaked under his weight. It's not that he was fat. He had less body fat than anybody I'd ever seen.

But he was big. Probably six four. With slabs of muscle everyplace it's possible to get muscle.

Weirdly, he had dimples. I know it's not logical, but to me, dimples didn't belong on a guy like Saunders. Yet there they were.

"Camp Wilderness philosophy. *My* philosophy."
Saunders said the words slowly. Like they tasted
good in his mouth. "I believe that your generation
has not been tested. You've had soft lives. You've
been given too much. And so you have tried to test
yourselves in other ways."

Saunders nailed me with a look. "You, Mr.
Neemy, tried to test yourself by joining a gang. I'm
sure that made you feel like a man. I'm sure you
think you've proven your strength and bravery."

"Hell, yeah," I answered. Trying to be 100 percent Steve. A guy with zero percent interest in
Saunders or his philosophy or his camp.

Saunders let the front legs of his chair fall back
to the ground with a thud. "There is no profanity
at Camp Wilderness. If you use it, you and your
bunkmates will run the hill with full packs. And
trust me, Mr. Neemy, your bunkmates won't
thank you for the opportunity to challenge themselves."

He turned to the girl. "And you, Miss Hanks,
you probably feel that you've tested your clever-
ness by creating computer viruses that take time
and money from hardworking people." She kept
her eyes on the bear.

"Mr. Moya, you might think that you've shown
the world how great you are by walking out of

stores with thousands of dollars of merchandise," Saunders continued. "But all of you are wrong. You haven't proven anything except your weakness."

Saunders stood up. He walked in front of his desk and began to pace. His heavy hiking boots made tracks in the fur of the rug.

"My philosophy is that children like you have been crying for a place to really test yourselves. To really see what you're made of. Camp Wilderness is that place. You'll have to push yourselves hard here. Harder than you would have believed was possible. I'll make you see the potential in yourselves. And when you see it, when you realize the strength inside you, you won't have to resort to gangs or stealing to show the world how important you think you are."

"I have no idea what you're talking about," Joe said.

"I'm sure you don't, Mr. Moya," Saunders answered. "But you will. I promise you that."

An image of Zack Maguire exploded into my head. Body twisted. Eyes vacant.

How hard had Saunders pushed him? Had he pushed Zack so hard that Zack was at the point of exhaustion that day on the mountain? Had Saunders basically caused Zack's accident?

SUSPECT PROFILE

Name: Linc Saunders

Hometown: Hannibal, Missouri

Physical description: 6'4", approximately 270 lbs.- most of it muscle, age 42, black hair, green eyes, full beard.

Occupation: Director of Camp Wilderness

Background: Worked as a guard at the Chillicothe Prison in Missouri before opening Camp Character and Camp Wilderness; never married, one son; B.A. in theater arts from the Rocky Mountain College in Montana.

Suspicious Behavior: Camp Character had to be closed because a teenager died there-one worker at the camp claimed Saunders was responsible.

Suspected of: The murder of Zack Maguire.

Possible motives: Zack wasn't athletic enough to make it through the program, so Saunders wanted him gone. Zack wasn't going to be one of Saunders's success stories, so Saunders wanted him dead.

Or was it clear that Zack wasn't going to be one of Saunders's success stories? Did Saunders think Zack would go back to robbing or hacking or whatever his thing was? Had that made Saunders so furious that he made sure Zack fell to his death?

Or did Saunders just hate the fact that Zack wasn't a hiking, canoeing, camping kind of guy? Did that equal a lack of steel in Saunders's book? Did he decide to off Zack just because Zack wasn't at all athletic or outdoorsy?

I watched Saunders as he moved on to listing the rules. Way too many rules.

Maybe Saunders didn't do anything at all, I reminded myself. Joe and I were here to figure out what happened to Zack. We would need a lot more facts before we could make that call.

Saunders finally wrapped up his list of rules. He picked up a walkie-talkie from his desk. "Smiley to the office," he said.

"Over," the answer came back. Along with that walkie-talkie crackle.

Less than a minute later, a guy who looked about twenty-one or twenty-two came into the office. He wore a plaid shirt that was nearly identical to the one Saunders was wearing. Except the guy's was blue and black plaid, and Saunders's was green and black plaid.

"Gentlemen, this is Will Smiley," Saunders said. "He's the commander of your bunk. When I'm not around, you should think of Smiley as me. Obey him the way you would me."

I smirked. It seemed like a moment where Steve would smirk, because he wasn't planning on obeying anybody. Smiley narrowed his eyes at me. "On your feet, gentlemen," he ordered.

Smiley led Joe and me to one of the bunks behind the cabin. Six guys were inside. "New meat. Steve Neemy." He pointed at me. "Brian Moya." He jerked his thumb toward Joe. "Where's Ken Purcell?"

"Still on latrine-cleaning duty," a short guy with wire-framed glasses answered.

Smiley shot a glance at his watch and frowned. "Unacceptable. There's not much time until lights out," he muttered. "You men fill these two in on what's expected of them. I'm going to go check on Mr. Purcell." He left, slamming the door of the cabin behind him.

I spotted my gear on one of the beds lined up across the room. I headed over and flopped down next to my gym bag. Joe stayed near the door.

"What do you think you're doing?" a guy with a blond buzz cut demanded.

"What does it look like I'm doing?" I kicked my

gym bag onto the floor so I could stretch out.

"You need to be stowing your gear in your foot-locker. And you need to be doing it now," Buzzcut said.

All the guys were watching me to see what I'd do. I didn't bother to sit up. "What's your name?" I asked. "I like to know who I'm talking to."

"It doesn't matter what my name is," Buzzcut answered. "Just do it."

"His name is James Riboli. I'm Andrew Cooper," the guy in the wire-frames said. He did a fast intro-duction of the rest of the guys—Russell, Tim, Charlie, Dylan.

"The deal is—if one of us screws up, we all get punished," Andrew said after he'd finished playing host. "Saunders is all about teamwork."

He picked up my gym bag. "Since there are forty thousand rules, you might not remember that one of them is keeping your personal space clean and neat. That means whatever's in here"—he gave the bag a shake—"goes in there." He nodded at the footlocker.

I fluffed my pillow and stayed where I was.

"Why aren't you getting up?" James demanded. "First day. First minute. And you're causing prob-lems. You aren't going to like the way we deal with guys who let down the team."

I might not like it. But I did want to find out what it was.

"Let me give you my philosophy on James. *M-y-y-y-y* philosophy." Andrew did a decent impression of Saunders. He also did a decent job of pulling James's attention off me.

"See, James had a birthday a few months ago," Andrew continued. "His second birthday at our little camp. And you know how many candles there were on his cake? Well, he didn't have a cake. But if he did, how many?" Andrew turned to the other guys.

"Eighteen," Tim, Charlie, Dylan, and Russell all answered.

"Eighteen. That's right. And eighteen is a very bad age to be in here. Because if you screw up—or your *team* screws up—you could get booted from this place. And for James, that means prison. So it's very important to James that we all do everything perfectly."

Interesting. James had been here for more than a year. That meant he was definitely at the camp at the same time Zack was. And according to Andrew, James was terrified of getting kicked out of Camp Wilderness and ending up in prison.

Could he have wanted Zack dead? Was Zack somehow messing things up for the team?

Joe and I had to consider every possibility. Saunders wasn't the only one at Camp Wilderness with a motive for murdering Zack.

Joe spoke up for the first time. "I thought when you screwed up here, you got the death penalty."

"What's that supposed to mean?" Russell asked.

I knew exactly what that was supposed to mean. Joe was getting ready to bring up Zack.

"And I'm Russell Barbour, in case you also like to know who you're talking to. First and last name," he added. I saw flashes of purple when he talked. Colored braces.

"Hey, I'm from around here," Joe answered. "Everyone knows Saunders helped that guy Zeke off that mountain."

"Zack," Andrew corrected.

"Whatever. What I want to know is what he did to make Saunders so angry. I don't want to leave here in a body bag," Joe said.

"Zack didn't tick Saunders off," Russell said. "Zack was Saunders's little pet monkey. Saunders *loved* Zack, because Zack reported back on everything that went on in this bunk. I, for one, am glad he's dead."

"Harsh," Tim said.

"You weren't even at the camp when Zack was here. You never had to deal with him as part of your team. Only James, Ken, and I did. So shut it," Russell snapped.

Okay, so Russell, James, and Ken—who was out cleaning toilets—were the only ones who knew Zack. Important info. I didn't really need to pay attention to Tim, Dylan, or Charlie.

"Zack died because he didn't have the guts for

40

this program," James said. "He was always slowing us down. Getting us punishments. A guy like him should never have been allowed into the woods. He should have been sentenced to the library. Except he would have enjoyed that too much."

Russell looked from me to Joe. "Saunders is going to need a new pet monkey with Zack gone. I wouldn't put it past him to put a mole in the bunk."

"Monkey. Mole. Make up your mind," Andrew joked.

Russell walked over to Joe. "You started asking questions pretty fast. Does Saunders want to know if we think he killed Zack? Is that why you're so curious about a guy you never met?"

"Can we spell 'paranoid'?" Andrew muttered.

"I can," Dylan offered.

"I'm curious because, like I said, I want to leave this place alive. I don't want to be like Zack," Joe answered.

"I think you want to be *exactly* like Zack. I think you're Saunders's new snitch." Russell was right in Joe's face now.

Could Russell be Zack's murderer? Would Russell be willing to kill a guy James thought was a snitch?

SUSPECT PROFILE

Name: Russell Barbour

Hometown: North Adams, Massachusetts

Physical description: 5'9", 140 lbs., age 16, red hair, blue eyes, freckles.

Occupation: Sentenced to Camp Wilderness

Background: Five arrests for arson, three convictions; only child; plays the drums.

Suspicious behavior: Gave Zack a bloody nose.

Suspected of: The murder of Zack Maguire.

Possible motives: Believed Zack was a snitch.

"I'm a snitch because I asked a question? Are you off your meds?" Joe asked.

Dylan and Andrew snickered.

"What did you do to get in here?" Russell demanded. Spittle flew out of his mouth with every word.

Joe stared at him.

Russell turned to the rest of the group. "See? He has to think about it. He's not one of us. He's

Saunders's new monkey." Russell's hands tightened into fists as he faced Joe again.

"Wait. What are you doing?" Andrew said. "You're the arsonist, remember? Five arrests. Three convictions. James is the one who is in here for assault. We all have to stick to our specialties, or it'll be chaos. Chaos, I tell you!"

It was cool of Andrew to try and keep the peace. But it didn't work. Russell didn't even glance in Andrew's direction. His attention was completely focused on Joe.

All I wanted to do was get up and jam myself between Russell and my brother. But I had to be Steve. Steve didn't have a brother in this bunk. Steve didn't care about anyone but himself.

I had to let Joe handle this on his own.

5.
MORE SUSPECTS

Russell's hot breath blasted into my face. Not a good feeling. Or smell. Part rubber from his purple braces. Part bad breath. Part vanilla toothpaste. Which somehow made the odor *so* much worse.

One more second and he's gonna start punching, I told myself. *So possibly, you should stop analyzing the components of his breath.*

And do—what?

Why had I lost that coin toss? Now I had to be Spud Boy. And Spuddy couldn't punch back. Or if he did, he'd have to punch like Chet. Which is pretty lame punching. No offense to the C man.

I decided my only shot was to try to outcrazy crazy, freaky, paranoid Russell. Which would take some big-time craziness. I started out by scratching my sides with both hands. Then I added in the sound effects. "Ooo-ooo! Eeee-eee! Eeee! Eeee! Eeee!"

Good thing I played a monkey in the second-grade school pageant, right?

Russell stared at me like I was deranged. Excellent.

I turned up the volume. I *ooo-ooo*ed so loud I thought Saunders might be able to hear me all the way in his office. I just wished someone was eating a banana so I could grab it.

"He's as crazy as you are, Russell," Andrew said.

Nice! My plan was working.

"No, he's just a good actor," Charlie disagreed.

James threw a pillow at my head. "Knock it off."

I loped over to Frank and started pulling invisible nits out of his hair. Or wait. Nits might just be the eggs. Anyway, I pretended to eat the what-chamacallits. The little bugs that live in monkey fur. I could tell Frank was trying not to laugh.

Andrew, Tim, Dylan, and Charlie *were* laughing. Even James, a guy who should be in Rage Anonymous with my friend Russell, smiled.

Russell scowled at me. But he hadn't followed me across the room. So I'd managed to escape being pummeled. For now, at least.

I patted my stomach to show I was full. Then I

headed over to the bed with my junk on it and started unloading the million pairs of boxers Aunt Trudy had packed into my footlocker.

"He didn't answer my question about what he did to get in here," Russell said. "Did anybody else notice that?"

"Why should he?" James asked. "And just so you don't burst a blood vessel, I saw him get out of a cop car. The cops brought him and Steve here."

"The cops could have been doing Saunders a favor. Making the monkey look like a nonmonkey," Russell muttered.

But he didn't have time to work himself back up into the spitting-all-over-my-face mad stage. Because unsmiling Smiley came in the door with a guy I figured was Ken Purcell. Ken was a guy Frank and I needed to get to know. He was at the camp when Zack died.

"Five minutes to lights out," Smiley announced. He jerked his head toward Andrew. "Why are you unpacking for Neemy?"

"Just bein' neighborly. I like to see myself as the Welcome Wagon." Andrew upended Frank's gym bag to show it was empty. "Yee-haw. Teamwork and everything."

"I didn't see teamwork here. I saw someone working. And someone sitting on his behind,"

Smiley answered. "I don't want to see it again. Now everybody in the sack. Lights out in four."

I stowed the rest of my gear, since Andrew wasn't welcome-wagoning me. Then I got into bed. Thirty seconds later, the lights went out.

What felt like another thirty seconds later, the lights were back on. "Out of the rack. Chow in thirty minutes," Smiley barked.

Was he serious? I checked the closest window. It was still dark outside.

I guess bad boys get up before the sun. Because everyone else climbed out of bed.

"And get your packs ready. We're hiking today, camping tonight," Smiley added.

Along with my bunkmates, I grabbed a shower (cold water only); brushed my teeth (I could smell Russell's vanilla paste from the opposite end of the long row of sinks); and loaded my backpack with water, food, and camping supplies. Then we hit the mess hall.

The good news? There were girls in the big open room. The bad news? The guys and girls ate at separate tables. I got to sit with the guys in my bunk. More of the team stuff. I guess they thought we'd bond if we never got out of one another's sight.

And it's working already. I'd say three, four

more decades of eating, showering, and sleeping on the same schedule, and Russell and I would be BFF. Best friends forever.

For now, I decided to try to make nice with Ken Purcell. I wanted to get his take on what had happened to Zack.

I took a bite of my oatmeal. It tasted like wet sawdust. Not that I've tasted wet sawdust. But it tasted the way I imagine wet sawdust would taste. "Is the food always this good?" I asked Ken.

Yeah, I know I wanted to find out about Zack, not the cuisine. But when you're undercover, you usually can't just ask what you want to ask. You have to kind of dance around it. Let the other guy think they've brought up the topic on their own.

Ken gave a grunt. He shoveled a spoonful of the oatmeal into his mouth. Then he spit half of it back out.

The oatmeal was bad. But I didn't think it was *that* bad.

"I knew she'd find a way," Ken said. He picked up the blob of cereal he'd just spit out.

Man. Was everyone in the bunk mental-health-challenged in some way?

Ken wiped the blob with his napkin, and I realized there was a piece of plastic underneath. And inside the plastic was a piece of paper that had been folded until it was the size of a fingernail.

"We're not supposed to have any contact with the girls," Ken explained as he smoothed out the note. "But if you're smart . . ." He grinned as he began to read.

"Anyone want to feel jealous?" he asked when he finished. "Anyone want to see what Janet wrote me?"

"Janet Russo? No way!" Andrew exclaimed.

"Oh, yes, my friend." Ken passed the note across the table.

"Which one is she?" I asked.

"The best-looking one in the place," Ken answered.

I scanned the tables and spotted a cute girl with her hair in a long braid staring at him. I figured that had to be Janet.

"Red shirt and braid?" I asked.

"That's her."

James snagged the note from Andrew. "I can't believe she wrote you this when Zack's only been dead for a few months. That's one cold-hearted chick."

"Yeah," Tim agreed. "Let the guy's body start to deteriorate a little first."

"She wasn't that into him." Ken grabbed the note back.

"You wish," James answered. "You were sniffing

around her the whole time they were together. And she wouldn't even look at you."

And the suspects keep on comin', I thought. I'd been sure Frank and I would spend our whole time here investigating Saunders. But yesterday it started to seem like Russell and James both had reasons to want Zack dead.

SUSPECT PROFILE

Name: Ken Purcell

Hometown: Toledo, Ohio

Physical description: 5'11", approximately 160 lbs., age 17, brown hair, brown eyes, scar on chin.

Occupation: Sentenced to Camp Wilderness

Background: One arrest, one conviction for forgery; father died when he was two; two stepfathers; six stepsiblings.

Suspicious behavior: Helped Zack get into his mountain-climbing harness the day Zack died.

Suspected of: The murder of Zack Maguire.

Possible motives: Zack was going out with the girl Ken wanted.

Now Ken. Could he have killed Zack to have a shot with that Janet girl?

"She was trying to figure out how to break up with him," Ken answered.

Wait. Had Janet and Ken gotten something going while Zack was still alive? Had she told him she wanted to break up with Zack?

Another thought hit me. Could Janet and Ken have teamed up to murder Zack? Had they *both* wanted him out of the way?

I took another look at Janet. She was laughing at something the girl next to her had just said. Hey, the girl next to her was Miss Hanks. Who'd have thunk *she* could be funny?

Anyway, Janet was laughing. And her blue eyes were all sparkly. And right then she didn't look like the kind of girl who could do anything bad to anyone.

But looks don't tell the real deal. Every kid in this place—well, except for me and Frank—had done something criminal. You couldn't tell it by eyeballing them. No one had "arsonist" or "thief" or whatever stamped on their forehead.

I wanted to follow up on the whole Janet slash Zack slash Ken love triangle deal. But it was time to hike. Ken was a middle-of-the-group hiker, and

I—Brian Moya, aka Spuddy—had to be all the way at the back. Which prevented much talking.

And guess who was back in the way back with me? Yep. Russell. I told you we were going to be BFF. Someday.

The mountain we were hiking up reminded me of the Outer Limits ski run. Except in reverse. I felt like I was climbing straight up instead of zooming straight down. Which would usually have gotten me breathing a little heavily. But since I was Brian, I made myself pant.

"Too bad," I said. Pant. "No girls." Pant. "On hike." Pant. Pant. "Anybody." Pant. "Else." Pant. "Managed to." Pant. "Hook up?" Pant. Pant. "Besides Ken?"

I figured even without Ken around I could still get some info. Don't ask me why I didn't see Russell's reaction coming.

"Saunders want." Wheeze. "To know?" Wheeze.

"No!" Pant. "Man!" Pant. "Just hoping." Pant. Pant. "Might get." Pant. "Lucky."

Russell didn't answer for a moment. I didn't know if it was because he needed all his air for wheezing. Or if he was deciding whether or not to trust me.

Finally, he started talk-wheezing again. "Some of the guys sneak out at night. Meet up with a girl. Zack was the only one who was all ga-ga. He actually thought he was in love."

Russell stopped and retied his shoe. Actually, he pretended to tie his shoe. The shoe was already tied. It was a maneuver that gave him about two seconds of rest. The guy really needed at least a fifteen-minute water and catch-your-breath break.

But that clearly wasn't on Saunders's agenda. He was at the head of the group of guys—no girls on the hike. And he was showing no mercy.

"Now Ken thinks he's in love too," Russell continued. His wheezes were coming in the middle of words now. Not just between them. "Don't know what it is about that Janet girl."

I was about to ask if Russell thought Ken and Janet were sneaking around behind Zack's back. But a miracle occurred before I could. Saunders actually called the group to a halt. We were about three-quarters of the way up the mountain.

Saunders strode back down the hill. He stopped when he was about in the middle of the straggling line of hikers. "Look down there," he ordered.

I looked. Off the left side of the trail was the sheer rock face of the mountain. The bottom was a long way down. We'd done some serious hiking.

"As many of you know, a young man was mountain climbing along that stretch of the face not too long ago. And he died down there," Saunders announced.

He was the kind of guy who would never have any use for a microphone. His voice boomed and echoed all on its own.

"The young man's name was Zack Maguire. He

was murdered by the members of his team."

Russell's head shot up. I stared at Saunders.

"He wasn't ready for the climb. He was exhausted. And exhaustion makes for mistakes," Saunders continued. "But Zack would have been ready for that climb if his team had been there for him."

Huh? I didn't see the logic in that.

"Every time Zack slowed down—on a hike like this one, for example—one of his teammates should have made sure he kept up the pace. Every time Zack slacked off on his assigned laps in the lake, one of his teammates should have made sure he finished them."

Saunders shook his head. "Instead of being there for Zack, his team murdered him."

I thought it was possible one of Zack's teammates *had* killed him. But not the way Saunders was saying. Not by neglecting to force Zack to become some kind of super-fit climb-any-mountain kind of guy.

I glanced over at Russell. He was staring down at the long drop to the ground. Was he thinking about what he had done? Was he thinking about how he made sure Zack fell—because he was so sure Zack was some kind of informant?

I couldn't tell. Russell didn't have the word "murderer" stamped on his forehead either. That was something Frank and I were going to have to find out about him. And Ken. And Janet. And Saunders.

"Let's have a minute of silence for Zack," Saunders said. "Let's use that time to think about what it means to be a real team member. If one of your teammates fails, that means you fail. Remember that. And remember that I have the option of booting an entire team out of this camp if one member isn't worthy."

Is anyone thinking about Zack? I wondered as the minute of silence began. *Or is everyone just thinking about keeping their own butt safe and out of juvie? Or jail,* I added to myself, thinking of James.

"All right! To the top of the mountain. Double time!" Saunders ordered.

Russell was clearly having trouble with single time. I let myself lag, staying even with him.

James dropped into step beside us. "You heard what Saunders said. You wet-butts are my responsibility. You screw up, I screw up," He reached out and gave Russell a shove.

"So let me give you a little pep talk." He shoved me forward. "Whichever of you two gets to the top last is going to get a lesson in teamwork tonight.

Something that will help motivate you."

Something like beat you bloody, I figured.

I knew what I had to do. James was one of our murder suspects. I needed to see exactly how far he would go tonight.

So I slowed down.

6.

ARE YOU IN?

Saunders stared at the last few guys struggling up the mountain. Joe was bringing up the rear.

"If you men don't make it up here in sixty seconds, you go down to the bottom and start over!" he shouted. He pulled out a stopwatch and clicked it.

Was he kidding? It had taken us almost five hours to reach the top.

I watched as Joe put on a burst of speed. I watched as he suddenly stopped and put his hands on his knees and lowered his head. Acting like he could hardly breathe. My gut twisted up.

I knew what Joe was doing. He was trying to enrage Zack's murderer. He was trying to see if being the kind of guy who couldn't keep up would make the killer take some kind of action. A dangerous maneuver. My brother is nothing if not brave.

"What am I seeing? WHAT. AM. I. SEEING?" James screamed. "Get your sorry butt up here, Moya."

"Time!" Saunders shouted.

Joe was the only guy who hadn't reached the top.

"Who are that boy's teammates?" Saunders asked.

Slowly, the guys in our bunk raised their hands. Dylan only raised his to the top of his shoulder.

"Clearly, your teammate needs your support. So all of you can escort him to the bottom of the mountain and back up here. Go, go, go!" Saunders ordered. "That means you, too, Smiley. Your men. Your responsibility."

I started down the hill. And walked straight past Joe. If his plan was going to work, I couldn't interfere. The other guys—even bunk peacemaker Andrew—blasted Joe all the way down the mountain. Calling him every name you've ever heard.

And Joe just took it. Gasping so hard he probably couldn't have said anything if he wanted to.

Smiley didn't add to the Joe-bashing. Brian-bashing, I mean. But he didn't do anything to stop it, either.

On the way back up, the group was mostly silent. Even for guys who were in good shape, the second trip up the mountain was hard.

And the fun didn't stop once we got back to the top. "Smiley, your team is responsible for dinner and digging latrine holes," Saunders bellowed when he saw us return. "And why don't we add kitchen prep to that as well?"

"Mr. Moya. Mr. Barbour. You start on the holes," Smiley snapped. "Mr. Jameson," he said, pointing to Dylan, "fires. The rest of you—chow prep. That means cleaning the fish the other men caught while we were traipsing back down and up the mountain."

Somehow I ended up as one of the fish guys. Ken groaned as he sat down next to me. "I thought my legs wouldn't start hurting until tomorrow."

"Steep grade. And a different set of muscles gets pounded going up and down," I commented.

"Saunders is a sadist," Ken said. "The only way I made it the second time was pretending Janet was waiting for me at the top. In a bikini."

"I need a Janet."

Ken sliced open the belly of a fish with one smooth stroke. He obviously had experience with a knife. "Don't even think about taking mine," he answered.

"I won't. Not as long as you're holding that blade," I told him. "But does she have a friend?"

"I would ask—but that's not how I want to spend my Janet time." Ken started working on another fish. "I still can't believe that she wants to be with me. When I got that note . . . It actually said that she'd been thinking about me the whole time she was with Zack."

"It still must have busted her up when he died," I said.

"I guess." He quickly corrected himself. "I mean, of course she didn't want him to end up like that. Lots of people kind of had meltdowns when it happened. Especially the girls. But some guys, too."

Ken shook his head. "I was there, you know. When it happened. I still see it sometimes, when I close my eyes. He fell right past me. His mouth was open. Like he wanted to scream. But no sound came out."

A shudder ripped through his body. Was he feeling guilty? Did he have anything to feel guilty about—besides wanting Zack's girlfriend? I didn't have enough info to say.

Andrew strolled over. "Fish. I need fish. I'm ready to start cooking. Bam! Bam!" Ken and I both stared at him. "Like that chef. Emeril? Bam!"

I had no idea what he was talking about.

"Never mind. Just hand over the fish you're done with," Andrew told us.

"You're gonna have to wait a minute. We just got started," Ken said.

"Well, pick up the pace." Andrew clapped his hands. "I don't want to serve Saunders his dinner late. I thought lava was going to start flowing out of his head this afternoon."

"I couldn't believe that stuff he spouted about Zack," Ken said.

"Yeah. I don't get how Zack could have been Saunders's favorite like Russell was saying." I slid a fish onto the "done" pile. "He didn't exactly sound broken up that Zack died. He sounded like he thought Zack practically deserved it."

"Russell's the kind of guy who always thinks something's going on behind his back," Andrew said. "He thought I was a snitch for about a second too."

Andrew sat down next to Ken. "You were here when Zack was. What do you think? Was he Saunders's ooo-ooo eee-eee monkey?"

"If he was, they both deserve Oscars," Ken answered. "Saunders acted like he hated Zack. And not just because Zack was always slowing the group down." Ken shoved a gutted fish into Andrew's hands.

Andrew dropped the fish and picked up a plate. "Ever seen one of these before?" He twisted the plate back and forth in his hands. "Use it."

"The big reason Saunders didn't like Zack was that Zack never kept his big mouth shut," Ken continued. "Zack always had a smart answer for everything. Or some better way to do something. Or some reason that Saunders's philosophy was stupid."

"Yeah, I can see why Saunders wouldn't have him as a pet," Andrew said. "That speech today . . . The way he used Zack's death to give everybody a kick in the pants . . ."

"He pretty much said Ken, Russell, and James killed Zack," I commented.

"Saunders has said that before. He loves using Zack as part of his little inspirational speeches," Ken said. "But he was glad Zack died."

Ken stared down at his fish as he continued. "No more Zack always questioning him. No more Zack refusing to believe Saunders's lies. Zack just didn't buy that how good you were at hiking and stuff had anything to do with how good you were as a person."

"That guy Brian was saying that some people think Saunders killed Zack. That he did it during the mountain climb so it would be easy to make it look like an accident." I added a fish to Andrew's plate.

"There were a lot of rumors like that right after Zack bought it," Ken agreed. "Supposedly Saunders had another camp out west. A girl died there. The girl's parents thought Saunders killed her—or at least pushed her so hard she died. But Saunders paid them off."

Interesting. Joe and I hadn't heard that Saunders paid off the girls' parents. Guilty conscience? Fear of prosecution? Actually feeling bad about what happened?

I wasn't sure. But I was sure it was interesting information.

"Here comes Smiley," Andrew warned. "He's not happy after that public scolding he got from Saunders. So mush, mush, mush! Or whatever you say to speed up fish gutters."

I thought Ken and I had been doing a decent job with the fish. But Smiley was all frowns when he stopped in front of us.

Joe had been doing hard duty as wimpy boy. It was my turn to get in the game. And that meant showing a little attitude.

"Smile, Smiley," I coaxed. "As my aunt would say—it's a waste not to show those pretty dimples."

That didn't get a smile out of him. "Pathetic," he

said, eyeing our pile of cleaned fish. "You men are an embarrassment," he said. "The whole team is an embarrassment."

"You mean *your* whole team?" I asked. Heaping on some more 'tude. "Doesn't that sort of mean you're not doing your job right?"

Andrew's mouth dropped open a little.

"Are you implying your failures are my fault?" Smiley demanded.

"Hey, I just got here. And I was up to the top of the mountain on time. I don't have any failures to worry about," I shot back.

"No failures." Smiley crouched down in front of me so he could look me in the eye. "You're not even out of high school and you've been arrested. You're half a step away from juvie. You don't consider that a failure?"

I shrugged.

Smiley pointed his finger in my face—giving me a good look at his hairy knuckles. "Boys like you disgust me," he said. "Linc Saunders has created a place where you can turn your life around. He's keeping you out of a juvenile detention center. And you don't appreciate it."

He pushed himself to his feet. "If dinner's late, the whole team will be giving me push-ups. I'm thinking at least five hundred," he called over his shoulder as he walked away. "And that's after our KP duty."

"Oh, nice, Neemy. I hope you had fun acting like The Rock or whoever it was you were channeling," Andrew burst out. "Now he's going to be dying to hand out the punishments."

"He already was," I answered. "We made him look bad in front of his god. What did Saunders do to make Smiley worship him like that?"

"Smiley has no spine of his own," James said, joining the group. "He needs a guy like Saunders to give him one. If he was out in the real world, and not a counselor in here, no one would ever listen to him."

James's theory kind of made sense.

"But in here, in Saunders's world, what he says goes. And Neemy just mouthed off to him," Andrew said. "So be prepared for push-ups if anything goes wrong."

"I'm not worried about Neemy right now," James told Andrew. "I want to know what we're going to do about Moya. We're not letting him get away with landing us that extra trip on the mountain without punishment."

"It's not like the guy messed us up on purpose. If you're not in shape, getting up the mountain is practically impossible," Andrew protested.

It's what I would have said. If I was Frank Hardy and not Steve Neemy. I was glad Joe had somebody sticking up for him.

"We can't let Moya think what happened today is acceptable," James insisted.

Ken nodded. He didn't look eager to dole out punishment, but he was with James.

"The next time, Saunders might not just assign us another trip up and down the mountain," James continued. "He might decide to boot us all. And I'm not ending up in jail because some kid can't cut it out here."

James turned to Andrew. "So are you in? Or are you part of my problem too?"

Andrew hesitated. Then he said, "I'm in."

"What about you, Neemy?" James asked.

There was only one answer to give. Joe had set this situation up. Now I had to let it play out.

"I'm in," I told him.

7.
A LESSON IN PAIN

I struggled to swallow a bite of my fish. It's not that it was bad. Somebody on my team could actually cook.

It's just that I was getting all these looks from the guys in my bunk. Looks that let me know something bad was going to happen. To me. And soon.

Well, it's not like I hadn't practically begged for it. But that didn't make this part of the plan any easier.

I tossed my paper plate—and most of the fish—into the campfire. The flames popped and crackled with the new fuel. Then I got up to use one of those holes I'd blistered my hands digging.

I heard a twig snap behind me. Was this it? Was I about to be ambushed on the way to the so-called toilet?

A second later I felt a hand on my arm. I jerked free and spun around.

And saw Frank.

"Your plan worked, little brother," he told me. "James has organized a 'lesson' for you. I'm not sure exactly what's supposed to happen. But it's happening tonight."

"Yeah, he pretty much told me that when I got you guys assigned that second hike," I answered.

"I think we need a signal. I'm not going to let things get too intense. But if you need help and I haven't moved in yet, just say—"

"Mommy?" I suggested. I forced a laugh.

"Do you always have to try and make a joke out of everything?" Frank burst out. "James could be the guy who killed Zack. And you've put yourself in his hands."

"But I have you for backup," I reminded Frank. And myself. It made me feel a little less twitchy. "We have to let James go far enough to see how far he's gonna go. Does that make sense?"

"Yeah." Frank rubbed the back of his neck. "I don't like it. But it makes sense."

"If I want you to come to the rescue, I'll just find a way to say 'Zack,'" I told him. "Now, do you mind? I need to be alone with a hole."

Frank disappeared into the darkness without

another word. I did what I had to do. Which, just so you know, involved leaves instead of nice, soft, quilted paper. Then I returned to the group.

The sight of all the guys around the campfire made the saliva in my mouth dry up. It could almost have been that photo in the newspaper article. That picture where Zack was grinning. Thinking everything was okay.

Not knowing he had almost no time left to live.

I returned to my spot next to Andrew. He didn't look at me when I sat down. Nobody wants to look at the next dead guy. Was that the deal?

You won't believe this. But while I was waiting to get pummeled into the ground—or whatever was going to happen—I had to sing.

I didn't see Saunders as the kind of guy who would promote singing around the campfire. But he did. He strode around the group, booming out corndog favorites like "Home on the Range." Expecting everyone to join in. Probably ready to make us all stumble up and down the mountain in the dark if we didn't. Loudly. With smiles on our faces.

At least I wasn't sitting close enough to Frank to hear his tonally challenged mooing.

Aw, who am I kidding? I wanted to be as close to Frank as possible tonight. But I was Brian Moya.

And Brian Moya had no reason to think Steve Neemy would be any kind of friend.

Finally, the torment was over. We were allowed to hit the sleeping bags. Someone had thoughtfully put all the rocks that I'd removed back under the square of plastic ground cover my bag was lying on.

Hey, if that's the best James could come up with, I'd have to take him off the suspect list. It was more of a fourth-grade maneuver. Ha-ha—you have to sleep on rocks.

I closed my eyes. Even though there was no way I would be able to fall asleep.

Except I did. A day of hiking and hole-digging will do that to you.

I was dreaming that I was a dog. And these dog-catchers were after me. I knew they were going to take me to the pound and gas me.

You don't need to have studied dream interpretation to figure that one out, right?

Anyway, the two dogcatchers kept whispering to each other. Then I kind of half woke up and realized the whispering was still going on. I think my brain had worked the whispers into my dream.

"I'll pull him out of the bag. You put the blindfold on."

I recognized the voice. James.

I figured I might as well pretend to still be asleep. My job tonight was to do nothing. And see what got done to me.

A moment later hands grabbed me by the shoulders and yanked. I slid right out of my sleeping bag. Then I was hauled to my feet.

Someone wrapped a blindfold around my eyes. From the smell, I think the blindfold was a couple of wool socks—socks that had been worn during a long hike—tied together.

"We have to gag him," someone said. Not sure who. "If he yells, we'll all be dead."

"Like Saunders didn't pretty much tell us to do this," James whispered.

But another sock found its way into my mouth. Bile rose up in my throat, and I had to swallow hard to get it back down.

I guess they figured Saunders wanted this to happen—but he didn't want to see it happen. So they gagged me to keep me from bringing him to the party.

Someone grabbed my arm. Somebody else put their hand on the back of my neck—but lightly.

Frank, I decided. Seemed like something he would do. Get in the middle of the action so he would be there fast if I needed him.

I was jerked forward. I couldn't stop myself

from stumbling a little. Blindfolds will do that to you.

"Move!" a voice I couldn't identify ordered.

"Will you shut it," Frank said. "Smiley is about four feet away from us." He was talking pretty loud for someone telling other people to be quiet.

I got another jerk on the arm. I walked as quickly as I could. I didn't want us to get stopped. Frank and I needed to see what these guys would do.

You know how they say your other senses get stronger if you lose one? Well, it's true. With the blindfold on, I could really taste the flavors of grunge on the sock in my mouth. I could really smell those toilet holes we were passing, too.

I hoped James hadn't decided to stuff me down one. That would be cruel and unusual. At least if you get a swirly at school, the water is somewhat clean. The holes out here had no water.

A tree branch slapped me in the face. We were clearly moving deeper into the woods.

Out of earshot.

The ground under my feet turned from hard and crunchy with twigs to smooth and sort of slick. I figured dewy grass. A clearing.

My arm was released. The hand disappeared from the back of my neck.

The silence was . . . it was loud. If you know what I mean. And the air felt charged. Like a storm was coming.

Somebody must have given a signal. Because a fist slammed into my stomach. Twice. Fast and hard.

I'd known this was coming for hours. But knowing doesn't really do anything to prepare you for the pain.

"This is what happens when you screw the team," James told me. "I am *not* taking a fall for you."

He must have been about to throw a punch, because Andrew said, "Don't touch his face. We don't want any questions."

I got another punch. In the kidneys. But it was a Frank punch. No pain. I gave an *ooof* anyway. To make Frank look good.

"Think of that when you get tired," Frank told me.

Something heavy—a tree branch?—slammed into my legs. Just behind the knees. I went down.

"Next time, you keep up. Or this is nothing," somebody said, and followed it up with a kick.

The kick shoved me across the grass. I felt a rock slice into my forehead. Hot blood began to drip down my cheek.

8.

KNOCKED OUT

Joe was bleeding. He hadn't given the code word for me to stop this. But he was *bleeding*.

James pointed at Andrew, then nodded at Joe. I saw a flash of uncertainty cross Andrew's face. But he pulled back his foot and aimed a kick at Joe's back.

"Wait!" I cried before the kick could connect. "I think I heard something."

"Saunders likes it when we handle things ourselves. He's not going to come out here," James said.

"But what about Smiley? He could have heard us. He could have followed us," Andrew answered. He looked anxiously over his shoulder.

I was almost positive Smiley *had* heard us. I'd

75

said his name as loudly as I could when we moved past him. But it looked to me like he was going to pretend to be asleep and let whatever would happen happen.

SUSPECT PROFILE

<u>Name</u>: Will Smiley

<u>Hometown</u>: Billings, Montana

<u>Physical description</u>: 6'2", approximately 230 lbs., age 22, brown hair, green eyes.

<u>Occupation</u>: Camp Wilderness Counselor

<u>Background</u>: Raised by single mom who never told him who his father was; no siblings; attended two years at Montana Tech, but didn't graduate.

<u>Suspicious behavior</u>: Handed out the gear the day of the mountain climb.

<u>Suspected of</u>: The murder of Zack Maguire.

<u>Possible motives</u>: Wanted to impress Saunders by having a perfect team—and that didn't include Zack. Or Saunders wanted Zack dead and Smiley did the dirty work.

"Smiley wants to *be* Saunders," James protested. "He's not going to do anything he thinks Saunders won't like. And, like I said, Saunders wants this. That's what his whole speech today was saying."

I didn't know if that was true or not. But I did know that if Saunders was a murder suspect, then Smiley should be too. Because I had the feeling that James was right. Smiley wanted to be Saunders. And that made him dangerous.

"No, I didn't mean I heard a person. It sounded more like a bear," I said.

"A bear?" Andrew backed away from Joe. He looked ready to run straight to his sleeping bag and cover his head.

"Yeah. Maine is full of black bears. But they don't usually attack," I said.

"Wait. Not *usually*?" Charlie asked. He sounded a little freaked. Good.

"A friend gave me the scoop on what to do when she found out I had to come here," I went on with a silent *thanks, Mom*. "If you see a bear, you're supposed to put your hands over your head and say something like, "'Oh, sweet brother bear, I didn't see you. I apologize for coming to your home and I will leave now.'"

"Huh?" James asked.

I shrugged. "I don't know anything about bears. I'm from Brooklyn. But that's what she told me."

"I see a bear, I'm shooting it," James announced.

"Oh, they let you bring a gun in here?" Andrew asked. "I figured with this being basically prison—"

"Shut it," James said.

"See, there it is again," I said. I shot a look at Joe. He was really still. Was he badly hurt? Or had he decided to be smart and lie low?

"Did you hear that? Something moving through the trees," I continued.

Ken stared down at Joe. "I think he's probably figured out we're serious."

Russell nodded. He probably didn't think he could say anything. That guy on the ground was almost him. He'd been almost as slow as Joe had.

"Okay, let's get back," James said. "He can find his own way."

"His head's bleeding," Dylan pointed out.

Thank you, Dylan.

"He's fine. It's just a trickle. Now, come on," James ordered.

And the group started moving out. Maybe some of them were afraid of what James would do to them if they didn't leave Joe.

I hesitated. Could Joe make it back okay on his

own? He could pull the blindfold off as soon as we left. But how bad was his injury?

As I tried to decide what to do, Joe opened his eyes. And winked at me.

I let out a breath I hadn't even realized I'd been holding. "I'm in no hurry to see a bear. If I get the urge, I'd rather go to the zoo," I said. And I followed James and the others back to camp.

But I couldn't stop thinking about how sure James was that Saunders would be all hunky-dory about what we'd done to Joe. I figured it was time for me to do a little more investigating of the guy we'd come here to investigate.

So the next day, instead of going to the mess hall with everyone else, I went to Saunders's office. He seemed surprised to see me. I guess not many guys show up there voluntarily.

"Mr. Neemy. I hope you enjoyed your first day here," Saunders greeted me. "I'm sure it was a challenge for you to take the mountain twice. But I have to say, you did admirably."

"Thanks."

He stepped back so I could enter his office. His body was big enough to block the whole doorway.

Wait. I was supposed to be the guy with attitude. And I'd just given Saunders a thank-you.

"You know what, though? I don't think surviving blisters on my feet has anything to do with the rest of my life."

Saunders's dimples disappeared along with his smile. "And that's what you came in here to say to me?"

"No." I sat down without being invited. Saunders stayed on his feet, all six-four of him towering over me. He raised an eyebrow.

"The guys in my bunk—me included—gave Brian Moya a beating last night," I blurted out. I wasn't sure how else to say it.

"Pretty much everyone thought that was what you'd want. But I wanted to ask you myself," I continued. "If you think that's the way things should be handled, then I think you should have the guts to say so."

My words came out pretty forceful. Probably because I really believed what I was saying. It was wrong for Saunders to let a bunch of teenagers do his dirty work. If that's what the deal was.

"And why would pretty much everyone have thought that's what I'd want?" Saunders asked. His face and his voice were expressionless.

"Duh. Did you listen to yourself?" I asked. "If someone on our team isn't doing enough laps or moving fast enough, then we're supposed to fix it."

Saunders crossed his arms over his chest. "And when did I talk about the beating?"

"How else are you supposed to get someone to do what you want them to do?" I asked.

"Inspiration. Motivation. Leading by example. Humor. Bribery." Saunders seemed to be enjoying his own words again.

I stood up. "I figured you wouldn't care. This was a waste. Who cares about Moya anyway?"

"Sit back down. You'll leave when you're excused," Saunders told me.

"You forgot to put 'court order' on your list of ways to get people to do what you want," I muttered. But I sat.

Saunders picked up his walkie-talkie. "Smiley. To the office. Now."

Less than a minute later, Smiley came through the door. "Neemy. I was looking for you. Why aren't you at chow?"

"Tell him," Saunders said. "Tell him what you told me."

"The guys and I took Moya into the woods last night. Taught him a lesson for making us do the mountain twice," I said. "Pretty much everybody thought it was what Saunders would want."

I gave the Steve Neemy trademarked shrug. "I decided to be sure. It wasn't exactly my style.

Whaling on some guy because he's too out of shape to climb a hill without practically stroking out."

"So you're not just a pathetic little tattletale. That's what you're saying?" Smiley asked.

"He did the right thing to come to me," Saunders asked. "What happened to Moya is absolutely unacceptable."

Was he saying what he had to say? Or did he mean it?

"I hold you responsible," Saunders told Smiley. "If you were any kind of leader, your men would never have behaved this way."

It definitely sounded like he meant it. Smiley must have thought so too. His face had turned pale under his tan.

"You, get to the mess hall," Saunders told me. "You're going to need all your energy today. Another hike."

"And you, out of my sight," Saunders ordered Smiley. "I can't stand to look at you. The men are here to learn how to deny their violent natures. They are here to stay out of gangs—not form new ones. Take control of your team. Or you won't have one much longer."

I decided to walk to the mess hall by way of the lake. It would only take a few more minutes. And I could use the time to think.

My gut was telling me that Saunders wasn't a murderer. He might have pushed Zack so hard that Zack had an accident. And if he did, I definitely thought he was partially responsible for Zack's death.

But I couldn't really picture Saunders killing someone. He had a weird kind of moral code. It was warped and twisted. But it was there.

Unless Saunders just had me totally snowed. I needed to talk to Joe. Compare notes. We hadn't managed to find a second by ourselves since I'd told him what James had planned.

Maybe we could meet in that boathouse, I thought as I started past the building.

That turned out to be my last thought for a while.

Something hard slammed into my head. Something warm and wet began to coat my scalp. Blood. Worms of light began wiggling across my vision.

Then everything went black.

When I came to, I was inside the boathouse.

And the boathouse was on fire.

9.
WHERE THERE'S SMOKE . . .

Where's Frank? I wondered as I sat down at the team table in the mess hall. He'd been with the group when we left the bunk, but he'd disappeared somewhere along the way.

I figured he'd explain all. Whenever we could find a time and place to talk.

"Oatmeal again. Yum, yum," I said. The bowls were at the table when we sat down. No choice. Eat it or starve.

Ken didn't seem to mind. He was rooting around in his with his spoon. Looking for another note, I was sure.

But I found one in my bowl before he found anything in his. Anything besides lumps, that is.

I dropped my spoon on the floor. Then I stood

up and headed for the kitchen to get a new one. I wanted to read the note in private.

"The five-second rule isn't good enough for you, Moya?" James called after me.

"One second on that floor is too long." Actually, the floor was fine to eat off of. Cleanliness was clearly a Saunders priority.

As soon as I was out of sight behind the kitchen doors I pulled my note out of its plastic casing. I couldn't believe what I was seeing. It was from Janet.

And she wanted to meet with me. Right now. By the latrines.

It's not like I was going to say no. "Gotta hit the head," I mumbled. Not that any of the kids doing kitchen duty seemed to care why I was in there or where I was going next. They had their own problems, I'm sure.

I ducked out of the kitchen's back door and trotted toward the latrines. I could see Janet waiting. What did she want? Was my bad-boy mojo heating up? Did she want to trade Ken in for me?

Janet grabbed my hand when I reached her. "Come on. I need to talk to you." She pulled me down a path that headed toward the lake. She stopped next to a little wooden bench that was almost hidden by a cluster of trees.

We sat down. I waited for her to say something. Because, hey, she's the one who called the meeting. But instead of talking, she started making these sniffling noises.

My gut lurched when I realized she was crying. I'm good in most situations. I've been held hostage. I've been shot at. I've been in a car chase. I've skied the Outer Limits. No problems. Well, not many.

But put me near a crying girl . . . and it's like my brain turns to marshmallows. What was I supposed to do here? I knew what I wanted to do—run.

Janet pulled in a long, shaky breath. "Sorry." She wiped her nose with the back of her hand. "Sorry," she said again.

"That's okay," I told her. It wasn't. But if I said it wasn't, she might start crying again.

"It's just . . . I used to meet Zack here. I haven't been here since . . ." Her green eyes got all wet and shiny. She was about to start up again. I could feel it.

"Yeah, uh, that must be hard," I mumbled.

"I didn't bring you out here to bawl all over you." Janet used both hands to sweep her long hair away from her face. I got a blast of flowery shampoo smell. "I heard what happened last night. The other guys taking you into the woods and—" She hesitated.

Geez. This girl knew I'd gotten pounded. That was totally humiliating.

"I was worried about you," Janet continued.

That made no sense. She didn't even know me. "I'm okay," I told her. I had bruises the size of grapefruits. But I was okay.

"You are now," Janet said. "But that's how it started with Zack. The guys harassing him. And then—" She shook her head. "This is stupid. I don't know what I'm talking about. I shouldn't be out here with you. Just be careful, okay?" She jumped to her feet.

"Wait." I caught her by the wrist. "Wait. Are you saying I should be worried I'm going to die like Zack did? What happened to him was an accident, wasn't it?"

I really wanted to hear her answer that question.

"Everyone was talking that night. People were saying that Saunders had killed Zack because Zack wasn't one of his model reform camp zombies."

"What did you think?"

"I didn't know what to think. I couldn't think. Zack was the only guy I ever loved—ever *will* love—and he was dead." Janet wiped her eyes with the backs of her hands.

I wished I had a handkerchief to give her. Aunt Trudy is always bugging me to carry a handkerchief. But it's not a guy thing. At least not in this century. Guys don't even carry Kleenex. I could offer her the use of my sleeve. That was about it.

"What do you think now?" I asked.

"I'm still not sure. Saunders isn't my favorite person in the world—but I'm not sure he would kill anyone," Janet answered. "He'd lay on the punishments. Push-ups. Midnight laps. Stuff like that. He might even boot someone to juvie if they made him angry enough."

"So are you telling me to watch out for someone else?" I asked.

"The guys in his bunk—your bunk—started hating Zack. He was always getting them in trouble. And they started doing things to get back at him. To try and get him in line."

"Like what they did to me last night."

Janet looked me in the eye for the first time. "Yeah. That's why I dragged you out here. To tell you it could get worse. Or maybe . . ." She looked away.

"Maybe what?" I urged.

Janet answered so quickly that her words ran into one another. "Sometimes I think Zack got killed because of me. Not because of any of the garbage with these so-called teammates."

She leaned forward and put her face in her hands. I gave her a pat on the back. Then I felt like an idiot. What did I think she was? A golden retriever?

"I'm sure you didn't have anything to do with Zack getting killed," I said.

And I was starting to really believe it. Unless Janet was playing me big-time, she'd been flattened by Zack's death.

The only thing I didn't get was her starting up something with Ken. Did she think another guy would help her get over Zack?

No, that couldn't be it. She was trying to hook up with Ken before Zack bought it.

"We should get back," Janet said. The last thing you need is for Smiley or Saunders or anybody to find you out here. Your team would end up climbing that mountain for a week straight."

I got up too, and we started back toward the mess tent. "Um, do you want me to give Ken a message or anything?" I asked. I didn't want to leave Janet without figuring out what was up with her and Ken.

Janet stopped and whipped around to face me. "What's that supposed to mean?"

I held up both hands. "Nothing. I just saw that

note you sent him. He passed it around to everybody. He was so psyched."

"I thought he'd keep it to himself. You must think I'm disgusting. Going after another guy when Zack's barely dead."

"I . . . I didn't think anything about it."

"Liar," Janet said.

"Some of the guys who knew Zack were a little surprised," I added. "But Ken told them that you were planning to break up with Zack all—"

"That's not true!" Janet burst out. "I loved Zack. We had all these plans for things to do when we got out of here."

The girl was truly confusing me. "But in the letter . . . You said in the letter that you'd been thinking about Ken the whole time you were with Zack."

"I hope I can trust you. I hope you can keep a secret," Janet said.

I tried to look trustworthy.

"The deal is that Ken has been into me since I got to this place, even after he knew I was with Zack. He wouldn't quit. No matter how many times I told him I had zero interest."

That cleared things up for me—not at all.

"I started thinking . . . and this could be totally stupid. But the way Ken looked the night Zack died. Maybe I'm crazy . . ."

She was definitely making me crazy. I had no idea what she was trying to say. "I'll definitely be able to keep your secret," I told her. "Because I have no clue what you're talking about."

Janet laughed. A real laugh this time. I liked the sound of it. Then her eyes darkened, and her expression turned all serious again.

"Ken looked happy the night Zack died. Pretty much everyone else was messed up that night. Or at least they were pretending to be. Even people who had never even said a word to Zack. Even people who had practically tortured him. But Ken—"

"Looked happy," I finished for her.

"Yeah. And the next day—the *next* day—he tried to get me to sneak out with him. Like now that Zack was gone, I would just move right on to him."

"But the letter—"

"The letter was a total lie, okay?" Janet exclaimed. "I couldn't stop thinking about how happy Ken looked. And then I started wondering if he wanted to be with me bad enough to . . . to, you know."

"Murder Zack."

"Yeah," Janet answered. "And I have to find out. I thought if I pretended like I was interested in him—and that I had been all along—he might confess. Brag about it, even."

Janet had formed her own little ATAC. With no Frank to back her up.

"Playing with a potential murderer. I think I should be the one telling *you* to be careful," I said.

"I don't care what happens to me. If Ken—or anybody else—killed Zack, I want to know. And I want to make them pay."

No more crying girl in distress. Janet looked ready to kick butt.

"I get that. But what about talking to the police, or—"

"Yeah. The police. I always love to have a chance to sit and chat with them." Janet sounded disgusted.

I'd forgotten for a minute who I was talking to. Janet didn't come to the camp to find romance. She'd been sentenced to a stay here.

"I get that, but—"

I forgot what I was going to say next. "Do you smell smoke?" I asked instead.

Janet took a couple of sniffs. "Yeah."

I scanned the sky. Spotted a geyser of smoke off to the left.

"Has to be the boathouse!" Janet exclaimed. "Come on!"

We raced toward the lake. "Help!" I heard someone cry in a smoke-clogged voice. "Help!"

My heart stopped, then began beating double-time. I recognized that voice.

"Someone's in there!" Janet yelled.

Yeah, my brother.

I pushed myself to run even faster. Janet and I rounded a corner and the boathouse came into sight. Orange-red flames ate away at its wooden wall.

"I'm here, Fr—" I stopped myself before I said his name. "I'm gonna get you out." I charged to the double doors.

No!

A length of chain secured by a padlock held the doors closed. Someone had locked Frank inside.

Windows! I tore to the side of the building. Chains and padlocks held the thick shutters in place over the windows.

"The windows on the other side are locked up too," Janet called, racing back to join me. "I'll run for help."

"No time," I barked.

Frank hadn't answered me when I told him I was out here. The silence was sending spikes of fear into my chest.

We needed something to use as a battering ram. What? What? What? I spotted a row of canoes tied to the dock in front of the boathouse.

Too light. They'd shatter before the boathouse

door wood. But we could use them for something else. "Come with me," I called to Janet.

I plunged straight into the lake and untied the closest canoe. I tipped it on its side. Let it fill with water.

Janet got it. She splashed into the lake next to me. Then the two of us struggled to pull the canoe out of the water.

The muscles in my arms screamed as we carried the canoe the few feet to the boathouse. Janet and I began to swing the canoe back and forth.

"One, two, *three*!" I yelled.

We let the water fly at the flaming front wall. The flames popped and sizzled but didn't come close to going out.

"More water!" I shouted. Janet and I lugged the canoe back to the lake. Tipped the canoe to fill it up again.

This was taking too long. It wasn't going to work.

Frank was going to die in there!

10.

BURIED ALIVE

I pulled in a breath. And got a combo of dirt and smoke that made me gag. Allowing more smoke and dirt into my mouth. And down my throat. And into my lungs.

The white worms were back. Squiggling across my line of vision.

You cannot pass out again, I told myself.

I jammed my fingers into the hole I'd started. The floor of the boathouse was earth. I figured if I had no doors and no windows, I had to make a tunnel.

I'd gotten about halfway under the back wall, which wasn't on fire yet. But time was running out. My chest was heaving. My lungs felt like they were burning hotter than the boathouse.

I felt cinders fall onto my back and head. The smell of my own hair smoldering was mixing in with the dirt and the smoke.

Was the roof on fire now? Was it going to crash down on me at any second?

Those thoughts were not helpful. And anyway, maybe I'd be buried alive before I burned to a crisp. My tunnel was barely wide enough to hold my body. There wasn't much air.

I inched forward. Digging, digging, digging. A splinter found its way under one of my fingernails, and a hot jab of pain went all the way up my arm.

You're feeling pain, that means you're conscious, I told myself. Conscious—good. Wham! Something hard hit my right calf. Something hard and hot. A piece of one of the ceiling beams. Had to be.

I jerked my leg and managed to throw the chunk of wood off me.

Not much time! Not much time! The thought was like getting zapped with an electrical current over and over.

I used my feet to shove myself farther into my hole as I dug with both hands. Something scraped down my back—the bottom of the wall I was tunneling under.

I could feel dirt turning to mud in my mouth. The smoke I'd inhaled was making me dizzy.

I had to rest. Just for a second. Just for one second.

Then I felt the ground slide out from under me. I was losing consciousness again.

No. Wait. The ground wasn't sliding away. I was sliding across the ground. Someone was pulling me. My hands were so battered by the digging that I hadn't felt someone grab them.

Then I was on my feet. There was light. And air. Still smoky. But cooler. I sucked in a lungful and gagged.

"A few steps. I need you to take a few steps," Joe told me.

I was standing in front of Joe! "How'd you know I was—"

"Move!" Joe gave me a shove. I stumbled forward. Just as a blazing section of wall crashed down behind me.

Joe hauled me over to the lake. Out of range of the collapsing building.

I pulled in another breath—and gagged. "How'd you know I was in there?" I asked, managing to finish my question this time.

"I wasn't looking for you, if that's what you're asking," Joe said. His face was streaked with soot, and his eyes were bloodshot. "I was having a nice time, sitting on a bench in the woods with a pretty girl."

I laughed. And it started me choking again. "You and a girl. I know you're lying."

"Like I was saying, I was there, with this pretty girl, and then I hear you yelling for help. . . . Well, after I saw the smoke," Joe said. "You don't have the best timing, man."

"What were you really doing?" I asked. I wiped my face with the back of my arm. All it did was smear the mud from my sleeve over my skin.

"Janet Russo was telling me to be careful. She thought I might end up like Zack," Joe told me. "But who cares about that right now? Who tried to torch you?"

I shook my head. And immediately regretted it. A billion hot needles dug into the backs of my eyeballs. At least that's what it felt like.

"Whoever it was hit me from behind." I gingerly touched the rock of flesh the rock of stone had made on the back of my head. "Knocked me out. I woke up to"—I gently tilted my head to the boathouse—"that."

Wait. The boathouse. "Shouldn't we be getting help? The whole forest could go up."

"Once we pulled you out, Janet ran for help. They should be—"

A siren's howl interrupted Joe.

"Here they are," he said.

A fire truck slowly cruised down the narrow dirt road that ran alongside the lake. An ambulance followed it.

I had a million more questions for Joe, but they'd have to wait. I was loaded onto a stretcher.

The last thing I saw as the paramedics carried me off was Saunders moving in on Joe. It looked like he had a million questions for my brother too.

I don't know how long it was before Joe made it into the infirmary to see me. The painkillers made time kind of . . . unimportant.

Joe sat down in the chair next to my bed. "I guess you haven't remembered who snuck up behind you and hit you on the head."

"The 'snuck up behind me' part made it kinda hard," I answered. "Because the sneaking. Is in back. Otherwise it's not snucking. Sneaking."

Joe nodded. "You okay?"

He looked so serious. Serious Joe. Serious, serious Joey. I hardly knew the guy.

"Yeah," I told him. "Thanks to you," I added, giving my head a shake. I reached for his hand. Because . . . it was good. He saved me.

Joe slid his chair back a foot. "Don't get all mushy," he ordered. "I had Janet crying on me today already."

"So what's her deal?" I asked. It seemed like

something Frank should ask. Would usually ask. And Frank was me. So I asked.

"Her deal is that she thinks her boyfriend was killed and she's playing Nancy Drew. Trying to figure it all out on her own."

"Nancy Drew. Cool girl. I like her car. And her hair," I said. "Strawberry yellow. Blond. Strawberry blond."

I realized I was still feeling a little . . . floaty. Everything felt kinda . . . nice. The sheets were so white. And the pillow was so soft. And—

I blinked a few times and tried to concentrate. "So . . . but where does that put her and what's-his-name? Ken. Kenny. Ken."

Joe looked over his shoulder. The room was empty. And sunny. Pretty sunshine.

"According to Janet—and I'm kinda wanting to believe her—she is playing Ken. She's just trying to get close to him because she thinks he might have murdered Zack."

"Because?" I knew I should be able to figure this out. But my brain was sort of . . . slow . . . right now.

"Because Ken wanted Janet for himself. And he knew she wouldn't go for him if Zack was in the game," Joe explained.

"It's about love. What percentage of murders do you think are about love?" I asked. "And how can something so beautiful cause so much falling off a mountain?"

"You are seriously starting to freak me out," Joe said. "Now focus. I don't want to have to slap you."

"I'm focus. I am focus," I told him.

"Let's talk about who probably did this to you. Before you slip off to la-la land."

I laughed. I knew the laugh made my throat hurt. But I couldn't feel it hurting my throat. You know?

"I would think Russell would be a likely choice. He's set a few fires in his day, you know?" Joe said. "But I couldn't come up with a motive for Russell, so—"

I pointed at myself. "I got it."

"Really?"

"Yep. I'm an amateur detective with my brother, remember?" I asked. I leaned toward Joe. "See, I'm not so doped that I forgot I wasn't supposed to say I was—you know. The alphabet thing. That starts with *A*."

"Yeah, I got you. And that's very important, the not talking about the alphabet thing. Remember that," Joe said. "So you know why Russell would want to flambé you?"

I closed my eyes. It helped me think better. Now

where had I put that? Oh, yeah. There it was. The motive.

"I went to talk to Saunders this a.m.," I said. "It's okay to say a.m. That's not the bad *A*."

I heard Joe give a long, loud sigh. "I wanted to see if he cared that those guys—and me, Steve Neemy—beat you up. And you know what? He did. He chewed Smiley out for letting it happen."

"Good to know. Useful," Joe said. "But Russell. Why—Oh. I get it. If Russell saw you talking to Saunders, he probably thought you were the snitch he's so paranoid about."

"Bingo!" I like that word. I said it again. "Bingo!"

"Right, bingo," Joe said. "I think we have ourselves a number-one suspect in Zack's murder. It's doubtful that there are two killers running loose. Even at Camp Juvenile Delinquent."

"Camp Juvenile Delinquent." I snorted. "You're funny."

"Thank you very much. I'll be here all week," Joe shot back. "As I was saying, I doubt there are two murderers. So if we're right about Russell torching the boathouse—"

"With me in it," I reminded him.

"With you in it," Joe repeated. "Then Russell is our most likely suspect for killing Zack. Janet was with me when the fire started. She has an alibi. Which puts her even lower on our list."

"Of who's been naughty or nice," I said. "I like Christmas," I added. Thinking about it made me smile.

"Right. So, you get some sleep—'cause Santa won't come if you're not sleeping," Joe said. "And I'll go spend some time with Russell."

There was something I wanted to say. Something important. Where did I put it? Oh, yeah.

"Be careful," I told my brother.

11.
YOU BETTER MAKE THE EFFORT

"So how's Steve?" Andrew asked when I returned to the bunk.

Everyone in the place was in bunk lockdown until Saunders figured out what had happened at the boathouse. I'd been allowed out to visit Frank because I'm the one who pulled him out of the fire.

"Steve is feeling no pain," I answered.

Usually I would have found it darn amusing to see Frank, aka Mr. Self-Control, all loopy. But considering he'd gotten that way on painkillers—after almost dying—not so much.

"What were you guys doing out at the boathouse anyway?" Ken asked.

I definitely didn't want to tell Ken that I'd actually been out there because I was having a little heart-to-heart with the girl he thought was his girlfriend.

Frank and I figured— Well, let's face it, I had to do most of the figuring. Anyway, we figured Russell was looking like a very good suspect. But Ken was a decent second.

I didn't want him coming after me because he thought I was after Janet. At least I didn't want that happening until I had Frank to watch my back.

"What aren't you telling us?" Russell demanded.

"I'm not telling you that I was in the woods to sneak a pee, okay?" I shot back. It was the first thing that popped into my head.

"If Saunders caught you peeing in a non-designated area, we'd be on KP duty forever," Andrew said. "He likes his rules."

"Yeah, that's why I didn't tell you. I don't need another lesson."

Andrew looked away. Like he was ashamed of what he'd done the night before.

James didn't look away. He glared right at me. "I think you do need another lesson. You better start thinking about what's good for the team. Not just what's good for you."

"It was good for my teammate Steve I was around," I answered. "The boathouse was locked tight. Someone wanted that guy dead." I looked over at Russell.

"Why are you looking at me?" Russell asked.

"Well, you were voted most likely to play with matches in the camp yearbook," Andrew commented. He took off his glasses and polished them on his shirt.

"So, what, I'm the only guy in the place who knows how to light a fire?" Russell raked his hands through his hair. "Unbelievable."

"Not so unbelievable," James said. "How many arson arrests have you had?"

Before Russell could answer, or launch into one of his spit-flying hissy fits, the bunk door swung open. Saunders and Smiley walked in.

Saunders gave Russell the hairy pointer finger. "Pack your gear. You have disgraced yourself. You have given up the privilege of being part of my program."

"The boathouse, right?" Russell punched the wall. "Of course, 'cause I set a fire once, of course I'm gonna do it again."

"Once?" James repeated softly.

Russell glared at him.

"Are you saying you feel unfairly treated?" Saunders asked him. "Are you saying I've misjudged you?"

"Hell, yeah, I am," Russell yelled.

"Show him," Saunders told Smiley.

Smiley pulled a piece of cloth from his pocket. Then he walked over to Russell's footlocker, opened it, and pulled out a shirt.

Same color as the piece of material. I think even Frank in his current state could have figured out where this was going.

Smiley held the strip of material up to the shirt. It wasn't exactly like putting a piece into a jigsaw puzzle, but it was close.

"We found this"—Smiley flapped the piece of cloth in Russell's face—"at the boathouse. Along with some footprints that match the tread and size of your hiking boots."

"You'll have a trial, of course," Saunders said. "But you won't be coming back here. This is a place for men who want to take charge of their lives and make a change. Start packing."

"I did not set that building on fire. If I had, I damn sure wouldn't have left a piece of my shirt behind," said Russell angrily.

Smiley grabbed a gym bag out of Russell's footlocker and started throwing stuff in. Less than two minutes later, Russell went bye-bye.

"And that's it. He's gone. He's in juvie." James dropped down on his bed and stared up at the ceiling.

"It's not like you actually care, is it?" Andrew asked him.

"That could be me. That could be any of us. Except, I'd be heading off to prison. Prison," James repeated dramatically.

"You don't really have to worry about it as long as you don't burn down any buildings," I told him.

James leaped off the bed. "You just don't get it, do you? That's not how it is here. Saunders is king. And the king can do what he wants. He can send me out of here because he doesn't like the smell of my socks."

"Wish I could," Andrew said. "Your socks are ripe."

I laughed. So did a couple of the other guys.

"You need to stop laughing," James told us. "You need to believe me when I tell you that if anyone does anything that puts me at risk, I will bring the apocalypse down on you. You heard Saunders the other day. He can and will toss an entire team if he feels like it."

James directed a lot of that little speech at me. And he kept on going. "Saunders booted a guy a while ago because he lost some swimming race. He didn't think the guy was being a good team player. Didn't think the guy put forth the effort. Well, everyone in this bunk is putting forth the effort on everything."

He walked over to me. Moved in close. At least he didn't spit the way Russell did. "You *better* make the effort," he told me. "Or you're going to end up with more than those few little bruises we gave you."

12.
RIDING THE WHITE WATER

"This is where it's all going to take place," Smiley said. "The Dead River."

The team was lined up next to our canoes. We'd lugged them from the camp vans over to the edge of the river.

"Tomorrow we race Grueber's team from this point down to the Forks, where the Kennebec meets up with the Dead," Smiley continued.

I couldn't help thinking back to the day Joe and I got our mission. The way he joked about ATAC giving us a vacation.

Even though I'd just gotten out of the infirmary, I was getting a little bit of vacation vibe. Joe's and my top suspect had been sent to juvie. And today we were forced to spend time on this awesome river.

Yep, I might want to do more investigating. But I couldn't. For the next few hours it was going to be all haystacks, sieves, holes, and waves. I couldn't wait to get paddling.

"I don't think I need to tell you that this team needs to win tomorrow," Smiley said. "This team has been a disgrace. This team needs to redeem itself."

This team? Or you? I thought.

"You'll be battling more white water per square mile than in any other river in the east." Smiley started pointing pairs of guys toward their canoes. "The dam's been released. So that will make things extra challenging. Are you up for the challenge?"

There were a few muttered "yeah"s. I didn't say anything. Steve wasn't an enthusiastic guy. I had to keep reminding myself not to smile. It was hard. More white water per square mile than any other river. How could you hear that and not want to grin like a maniac?

Smiley pointed Joe and James to a canoe. That wasn't going to be fun for my brother. But maybe he'd find out something worth knowing. Like whether or not James should still be on our list of suspects.

"I said, are you up for the challenge?" Smiley bellowed.

He got a slightly louder response. Only slightly.

Smiley scowled. He was clearly angry. But what was he going to do? Assign us push-ups for "yeah"ing too softly?

"You'd better be. If we lose, you'll all be getting up an hour earlier for a nice morning run."

That got a response. Some nice loud moans.

Smiley slapped a life jacket into my hands. "You and I will have to pair up. I'm putting you new boys with experienced paddlers until I see how you handle yourselves. Tim, you're strong enough to go solo."

Getting buddied up with Smiley lowered my vacation vibe a bit. But just a bit. 'Cause this river—it was just begging me to play.

"Okay, let's do this. Remember the scouting we did. Run hard. Run fast."

Smiley and I got our canoe into the water. Leading the group. Almost immediately the river narrowed. A wall of rock came up on the right. Not something you'd want to hit.

I knew we had about a third of a mile before we plunged into a pool. And oh, yeah! Here was the wave train leading up to it.

"Saunders is going to be so proud of the team if we win this thing," Smiley shouted. It was hard to hear him over the rushing water.

He glanced at me over his shoulder. I nodded. I couldn't believe the guy was trying to have a conversation now. Whoops!

My stomach bounced up to my throat as we dropped down into the pool. The next thing we had to do was catch the eddy that would be coming up on the right.

"A win would really make him forget about Russell. And about that fiasco on the mountain," Smiley continued. The muscles in his throat had to be aching. He had to scream every word.

I ignored him. If we missed the eddy, we could crash into a nasty boulder.

Here it comes, here it comes. And—got it.

We flew forward. The river widened. My eyes whipped back and forth. I wanted to take in everything. Yeah, *there* was the spume of white water I was looking for. "Hole coming up river left," I called to Smiley.

The canoe bucked like a bronco when we hit it. What a ride!

We swept down the pour-over. Smiley and I both paddled hard to maneuver the wide eddy that met us at the bottom.

And suddenly we were in the section of the river people call the minefield. Ranked Class III+ on the International Scale of Difficulty. Which means high, irregular waves. Lots of maneuvering necessary.

I hoped Smiley had stopped thinking about Smiley and started thinking about the Dead River. Because here came some haystacks—waves that pretty much stood still. Caused by obstacles on the river bottom.

I think I actually let out an un-Steve-like "Whee!" I couldn't help it. It was like a water roller coaster. Leading to a big, trashy hole.

Paddle, paddle, paddle, I ordered myself. We slalomed around the big, bad hole and around some smaller ones, then hit another pour-over.

We pulled right to enter the pinball section of the river. The name pretty much says it all. We were knocked around like one of the metal balls in an old machine. Ding!

Then the Dead gave us a little bit of a break. We were still shooting rapids, but they weren't as intense. But they got whiter with every few feet.

I spotted the big boulder that had been painted red. I remembered it from the hours we'd spent scouting the river before we put the canoes in. This was the start of Upper Popular Hill Falls.

I knew there was a hole at the bottom on this section. A hole that was as wide as the river. We needed to punch it.

And punch it we did! Then we were riding the wave train of Popular Hill Falls.

Way too soon it was over. What a run.

Smiley and I got our canoe out of the water. "I wish Saunders could have seen that!" he exclaimed.

I looked back up the river. Here came Tim. Perfect. Now Andrew and Ken. Ouch! They cartwheeled about five times coming toward us. But they didn't capsize.

Charlie and Dylan's canoe came next. That just left Joe and James.

Where were they? The current was so strong. It's not like they could really slow down. Even if they wanted to.

There! I saw the canoe.

My body turned cold.

I saw the canoe. But it was empty.

It flipped over. And I saw the hole in the bottom.

13.
DROWNING

Water slammed down on me, pinning me to the bottom of the river. My life vest was about to get swept away. Somehow it had slid off one of my arms.

My lungs ached. I couldn't see anything. I struggled in the direction I thought was up.

But the water was too powerful. It pushed me down with more force than I could fight.

Then suddenly the fight got easier. There was a force pulling me up. Battling the downward push of the water.

Frank. My brother had me by the back of my shirt. I could see his legs kicking as he worked to bring us both to the surface.

Just seeing him gave me back some strength. I

whipped my legs back and forth, adding to Frank's effort.

We surfaced. Nothing has looked as good as the sun. Nothing has felt as good as air moving into my lungs.

"If you wanted to go swimming, you should have worn a wet suit," Frank gasped. "This water is *cold.*"

"Just the way I like it," I answered through my chattering teeth. "Plus, now I can use some of that extra underwear. I didn't want to have brought it for nothing."

There was no point in trying to go against the water. Frank kept his grip on me as we were swept down the rapids of Popular Hill Falls.

When the white water went dark, we swam over to the shore. Well, Frank did most of the swimming. But I helped a little.

"Nice job, Moya," Smiley said as soon as I pulled myself onto the bank.

"Where's James?" I asked.

Smiley pointed to the opposite shore. A couple of the guys had gotten James out of the water.

"What happened?" Frank asked.

"Incompetence happened," Smiley answered. "Lack of strength happened. Lack of wit."

"What happened?" Frank repeated, ignoring him.

"I don't know. We were doing fine. Then we started taking on water. Lots of it," I answered. "We were trying to bail and maneuver the haystacks at the same time. And you know the rest."

"Get yourselves and your canoes to the van rendezvous point," Smiley ordered. "We're going to do another run."

"You've got to be kidding," Andrew muttered. For the first time, I noticed he was soaked. He'd obviously been part of the rescue squad.

Actually, all the guys had, I realized. Smiley was so twisted up about James and my bad performance that he didn't realize every guy out here had acted like part of the team.

I wondered if James would have jumped into the river to save one of the other guys if the situation had been reversed. I wasn't sure that was the kind of teamwork he cared about.

"You heard me," Smiley called. "Move. Get the canoes to the vans."

"Uh, my canoe has gone missing," I said.

"I'm aware of that," Smiley answered. "You and James will have to wait out the next run. Even though you two clearly need more practice than anyone else."

I managed to get myself to my feet. The muscles

in my legs felt like they had been turned into wet laundry. Heavy and cold. Useless.

I realized that my life vest was still looped over one of my arms. I yanked the sodden thing off. And that's when it hit me. The right shoulder strap was split in half.

I ran my fingers over it. The webbing on either side of the split felt rough.

I took a closer look. It was like someone had flayed the strap with a knife. It was probably almost ready to break when I put the vest on. The webbing holding the buckles in place had been messed with too.

Suddenly I felt ten times colder than I had at the bottom of the river. I knew in my gut that whoever had done this to my vest had also made sure that the canoe was primed to spring a leak while it was going down the rapids.

Someone had just tried to kill me.

I tried to remember how I'd gotten the life vest. It had been in the canoe. And it had been James's job to put all the vests into the canoes.

But James hadn't assigned me to the canoe. Smiley had.

I closed my eyes, trying to picture myself standing on the bank. Had James maneuvered me next to the canoe? Because I had ended up in the one I was standing the closest to.

Had James stood near me so that we'd get put in the canoe together? Did he want be in the canoe to make absolutely sure the hole he'd started—if it was him—actually broke open?

If he had, it would have put him in jeopardy too. But not that much. *His* life vest was fine. I could see it on him right now. A nice, tight fit.

The image of myself on the shore by the canoes wouldn't come clear. I hadn't been on guard. I'd been cocky. Thinking that Frank and I knew who the murderer was: Russell. And that he wasn't anywhere near the camp.

I'd been figuring Frank and I had more evidence gathering to do. But I'd been way too sure the truly dangerous part of our mission was over.

Rookie mistake.

The guys started hoisting their canoes onto their shoulders. I grabbed the back half of Tim's, and we started down the path leading to the road. My thoughts were coming so fast and so jumbled I could hardly keep track of them.

But I kept coming back to the fact that someone had tried to kill me.

And someone had tried to kill Frank.

I still figured there was only one murderer at the camp. But who would want me and Frank dead? Me and Frank and Zack?

Had someone figured out that Frank and I were fakes? That we were at the camp to find out what had happened to Zack? Had someone been afraid that we would find out the truth?

Nah. The cover ATAC had provided was rock solid. Even the cops who'd escorted us here thought we were true bad boys sentenced to the camp.

So me, Frank, Zack. Or Brian, Steve, Zack. What did we have in common?

Zack and I—Brian—were both spuddy, out-of-shape guys who slowed down the team. Brought down the punishments everyone hated.

But Steve/Frank was a total athlete. He was a guy you'd want on your team. You could count on him not to lag behind. To pull his weight.

He had attitude. And Janet had said that Zack wouldn't be one of Saunders' zombies. So Steve/Frank had that in common with Zack.

But I'd been reasonably zombie-esque, I thought, as we reached the vans.

What is it? I thought as I climbed inside the closest one. There had to be something that connected me, Frank, and Zack. But I couldn't see it.

Nothing came to me during the fifteen-mile ride back to the head of the run. And after that I had James to contend with.

The minute Smiley and the rest of the team left

for the second rapids run, he was on me.

"I don't know what happened out there," he said. "But however you screwed up, it better not happen again. Because we are *not* losing that race tomorrow."

I stripped off my shirt and put on one of the Camp Wilderness sweatshirts piled in the corner of the van.

"Are you listening to me?" James demanded. "I'm not going to prison because you screw up. And if we lose, we could all get booted."

He paused to suck in a breath, then kept on ranting. "I'm serious. Saunders is that crazy. He might just decide that men who can't win a race aren't men who should be here. We could be packing our bags this time tomorrow. Are you listening to me?"

"I'm listening," I snapped. "I don't really want to be, but I am. And you know what? Even if you kept your mouth shut, I'd probably try pretty hard not to drown again tomorrow."

James stretched out on the seat all the way in the back. "I'm gonna rest up. Get my energy up for tomorrow. I suggest you do the same."

I decided to ignore his suggestion. I decided it was time for a little investigation.

I waited until James's breathing was deep and

even. Then I grabbed his backpack. Unzipped it. Slowly, slowly, slowly. The sound felt as shrill as fingernails on a chalkboard. But James didn't twitch.

Okay, so, what did we have?

Bottled water. A box of raisins. An extra pair of socks—now soaked. Aw, did James have an Aunt T too?

And last but not least, a little notebook. I flipped it open. The same words were written over and over again. "I will not go to prison. I will not go to prison. I will not go to prison."

That told me exactly nothing new about James. It was clear to anybody who came within a mile of the guy that he was terrified of prison. Or what I like to call the Big House. It just sounds friendlier.

I ran my hands over the outside pockets of the pack. Nada.

I'd been hoping for a nice piece of solid evidence. Like whatever it was that had been used to mangle my life vest. But nada.

Still, it's not like I had searched everywhere. Should I risk it?

Definitely. That's what I was here for.

I crept down to the seat where James lay. His windbreaker had two pockets. *And what's in Pocket Number One?* the game show host in my head asked.

It wasn't a brand-new car. It was a stick of gum. Cherry. I thought about chewing it. The rest of the team was going to eat when they hit the bottom of the run. While James and I got zippo.

But I'm one of the good guys. So I put the gum back.

I studied the second pocket. James was lying half on top of it. Tricky.

But there might be something very interesting in Pocket Number Two.

I flexed my fingers. I was goin' in. Gently, I inched my fingers into the pocket. The nylon crackled. I knew the sound was soft. Softer than the zipper opening. But it felt like somebody had started to scream.

"You looking for this?"

James whipped a knife out of his sock.

He shoved me to the ground. Jammed one knee into my chest. And placed the knife blade against my throat.

This was no time to play Spuddy. I slammed my knee into James's belly. He wasn't expecting that from me.

I tried to roll away from him. There was no room on the floor.

Biting isn't my first choice in a fight. But I'm not proud. I twisted my head down and clamped my teeth down on James's wrist. Until he dropped the knife.

I managed to grab it. "If you were so worried about going to prison, you shouldn't have tried to kill me," I yelled. "Now I've got evidence. You're going down."

"What are you talking about?"

"You know. My life vest. You flayed the webbing with this knife," I shot back. "I don't know what you used on the canoe. But I'll find out."

James's eyes widened. He sat back, easing his knee off my chest. "You're serious? You think somebody tried to kill you?"

I wriggled free and grabbed my life vest. I hurled it at James. "Does this bring back your memory?"

James ran one finger over the split strap. "I didn't do this, man."

I grabbed James's life vest and flicked the knife back and forth over a piece of webbing. The damage looked familiar. From my vest.

"I'm not the only one who could have a knife like that. It's what we used on the fish," James protested. "They're easy to swipe. I kept mine, just in case."

"In case of what? Anyway, you can tell it to Smiley and Saunders. And the cops," I said.

"No. Please. You know what they'll do to me. A guy with my record," James said in a rush.

I stared at him. I'd found the knife on him. But he was right. The knife was exactly like the ones we'd used on the fish. And it had been pretty easy to keep. No one had really been watching us with them.

"I'll help you figure out who did it. Just give me a chance. I have an idea, even. Really."

"What's your idea?" I asked.

14.
BAIT

Keep your mind on the course, I told myself.

But I kept slipping into autopilot as Smiley and I swept over the haystacks and down the pour-overs. Because I couldn't stop thinking about Joe.

Was he alone with a killer right now? His canoe had been sabotaged. And I'd seen the way his life vest had been tampered with.

Was the murderer getting ready to try again while I was out on the river?

"Paddle, paddle, paddle!" Smiley yelled.

I realized we were heading toward a boulder. I stroked until my arms ached to get around it. From that point on, I managed to keep my brain where it needed to be. On the river.

But once I was on dry land again, I immediately went back to thinking about what had happened to Joe. The motives of the camp killer were making me nuts. I couldn't come up with a reason why one person would want me, Joe, and Zack dead.

Could there be two murderers at Camp Wilderness? It wasn't totally impossible. Just not that logical. Not that murder is always logical. In fact, most of the time it isn't. Killing is usually all about emotion.

So I should be trying to feel the feelings of the killer. Or killers. Not figure out the logic behind the murders—and attempted murders.

Easier said than done. At dinner in the mess hall, I still hadn't managed it.

"Lookie, lookie what I got," Ken exclaimed, pulling me away from my thoughts. He slid a note wrapped in plastic out of his mashed potatoes. The grin on his face was so big, *he* should have been named Smiley.

But his expression turned sour as he read the note.

"What's the deal?" Andrew asked. "She breaking up with you?"

"Are you insane?" Ken answered. "The whole letter is about how she thinks about me all the time. And how she wants to sneak out and meet me."

"Well, I can see why that would make you look like you just ate a pile of mouse poop." Andrew reached over and snatched the note out of Ken's hands.

"'Dear Ken,'" Andrew read aloud. "'I miss you so much—even though you're probably reading this just across the mess hall from me.'"

Frank glanced toward the girls' table. Janet was looking at his team's table. But Frank noticed she was looking at Joe, not Ken. Huh.

"'I think about you all the time.'" Andrew started making his voice all high and girly. "'It's the only thing that keeps me going in this horrible place. I can't wait until we're both out of here, and we can be together as much as we want.'"

"Isn't that sweet," James muttered. "But it sounds kinda familiar. Wasn't that in a letter to Zack?"

"She'd never have written anything like that to Zack," Ken told him. "She just hung out with Zack out of pity. She felt bad for him because he could hardly take a step without wheezing or tripping over his feet."

"'I'll try to dream about you tonight,'" Andrew went on reading. "'You try to dream about me, too. That way we can be together. Love, Janet. P.S. Be nice to Brian for me.'"

Ken took the note back from Andrew and glared at Joe. "What's the deal with *that*, Brian?" he demanded. "How does Janet even know your name? That's what I want to know."

"She helped me try and put out the boathouse fire," Joe answered.

"But why were you at the boathouse together?" Ken's eyes narrowed.

"Yeah, you should have both been at chow," James said. "Did you sneak off for a little slobber exchange?"

"We weren't at the boathouse together. We ended up there together. We both ran toward the smoke," Joe explained.

Ken did not look happy. He turned to the other guys at the table. "What do you think? A girl doesn't just say be nice to whoever if she's not interested in whoever. Am I right?"

"I think you're right," Tim said.

"Like either of you are such experts on girls," James commented. "Although—"

"Although what?"

"I've been getting to know someone myself," James said. "Somebody on Janet's team. And she did mention that Janet's always talking about our boy Brian."

"What girl? What's her name? Exactly what did she say?" Ken burst out.

"I don't really listen that much," James asked. "I just kind of nod until she's ready to stop talking. But I can see it. Janet's always looking at him."

"What? When?" Ken was halfway out of his seat.

"A couple of minutes ago. And the other day." James spooned a heap of mashed potatoes into his mouth. He seemed happy with himself. Like he was enjoying causing problems.

Ken jerked his head toward Janet. She wasn't looking at him or Joe. She was listening intently to something the girl next to her was saying.

Then they *both* looked at Joe.

A dark, angry flush shot up Ken's neck and splashed his cheeks. He looked ready to stroke out.

"She can't be interested in Moya. He can't even climb a hill," I threw out. "He's a wimp," I added, thinking of Playback.

I expected my comment to calm Ken down a little. Instead, he turned to me.

"And who do *you* think she'd be interested in? You!" he burst out, looking right at me. "I know you're interested in her. I've seen you checking her out. Since day one."

The guy was insane. But insane enough to kill

someone? That's the question I asked Joe when I managed to get a second alone with him after dinner. In the latrine. For some reason, this mission was all about meeting in bathrooms.

"Is he insane enough to kill?" Joe repeated. "Well, James thinks so."

"James? You talked about our case with James?" The top rule of ATAC was secrecy. Joe knew that.

"Not exactly. I accused him of trying to kill me. Long story short—I found a knife in his sock. Well, I sort of found it," Joe explained. Sort of explained. "The knife looked like it was the one used on my life vest strap."

"So why aren't we taking James in?" I asked.

"Because he begged me to give him a chance. And I thought I should. I don't want somebody going to jail who doesn't deserve it."

"So he begged. That's it?" I didn't like the sound of that.

"He told me he'd help me find the guy who tried to kill me. I didn't talk to him about Zack. Or you," Joe said. "He thinks it's Ken."

"If he thinks it's Ken, why was he practically inviting Ken to go after you?" I asked.

"Because that was the plan. If Ken tries to kill me again—case closed." He scratched the mosquito bite on his earlobe. "It's not like we didn't have Ken on our own suspect list. I can sort of see him going after Zack. Zack was stopping him from hanging out with Janet."

"Just by being alive," I agreed.

"Yeah. But there's a piece that doesn't make sense." Joe scratched the bite again. "Janet is acting like she's completely into Ken right now. Saying she misses him. Wanting to meet up with him. Making plans. Granted, it's because she's trying to see if Ken killed Zack—at least that's what she told me—but still."

"All right—but bringing you up in a letter? And being out in the boathouse with you? And looking at you," I reminded him.

"Right. So I'm sort of a threat. Nowhere near a Double Black Diamond kind of danger, but still a threat," Joe said. "But if Ken's our guy, he went after you, too. And you're like a bunny-trail-level problem. If that."

"Unless she likes really athletic guys," I joked. "I guess Ken could have to bake me in the boathouse because he knew after my performance hiking the mountain that Janet would be all over me."

"It doesn't make much sense, does it?" Joe asked. "Maybe we do need to think about two different murderers."

"Or one with zero logic," I said. "I was thinking

today that a lot of killing comes out of emotions getting out of control. Maybe the lack of logic just means we have a murderer who is hyper-emotional."

"Ken is definitely that," Joe said. "I mean, he clearly got all obsessive over Janet without any encouragement from her."

I nodded. "But there's obsessive, and then there's *obsessive*."

"We'll know for sure soon enough. James is about to put me on the hook," Joe said.

"All I can say to that is—huh?"

"Worm. Bait," Joe told me. As if that explained everything. "James is going to tell Ken that he found out I'm meeting up with Janet at that bench in the woods. Tonight. At midnight. If Ken comes after me and tries to—"

I didn't let Joe finish. "I'll be there to see it," I promised. "And to stop it."

15.
GO TIME

"You will do your best tomorrow," Smiley said. "You will find your core of steel."

I flashed on James's little notebook. The words "I will not go to prison" written over and over again.

Smiley was doing sort of the same thing. He seemed to think if he told us that we would win enough times it would happen.

"I'm gonna call lights out in a minute," Smiley continued. "And here's what I want you to do. I want you to picture the river course in your mind. The Minefield. The Pinball. The Humpty-Dumpty. The Elephant's Foot."

Smiley walked down the row of beds, taking a moment to speak directly to each of us. Except me.

He didn't even glance at me. I guess I was a lost cause to him. Hopeless.

"I want you to picture every boulder, every haystack, every wave. And I want you to picture yourself triumphing over every single obstacle."

Smiley sat down on Russell's empty bed. "You might think that I don't know anything about your lives. You might think I don't know anything about real obstacles. Things besides boulders in a river. Or a steep hill."

He stared down at his clasped hands. "But I do. For starters, I never even knew my dad." He gave a bark of laughter. "My mom wasn't even sure who he was. *That* was an obstacle."

Smiley's head jerked back. Like someone had given him a light punch in the chin. He blinked. And he seemed to realized he'd just been talking to us like an actual person. Not a counselor zombie.

"Five to lights out." He stood up and positioned himself by the light switch, clearly planning to stay there until he had to flick it. A good zombie.

I changed into pajamas, making sure my pants, sweatshirt, and shoes were all within easy reach at the top of my footlocker. I'd be going out again soon.

Smiley called lights out. My go time was eleven forty-five. I had a few hours to think. The camp was definitely in early-to-bed-early-to-rise land.

I used the time to do some visualizing. But not of the river ride. I pictured myself sneaking out of the cabin without waking anybody up. I pictured myself creeping out to that bench in the woods.

I pictured Ken leaping out of the trees. I pictured a knife in his hand. Coming down at me.

I pictured Frank grabbing Ken's hand. I pictured the knife stopped inches away from my chest. Make that a foot, I told my brain. I readjusted the image.

I pictured Frank and myself testifying against Ken. I pictured our dad smiling. Seeing that we had closed the case—even though we hadn't discussed it with him.

When I reached that moment, I rewound and replayed. I knew some professional athletes did a lot of visualizing. Seeing themselves crossing a finish line or performing a superior slam dunk.

I figured it couldn't hurt. And I didn't have anything else to do.

I definitely couldn't sleep.

So I played director with my little head movie. Improving the colors. The sound effects. The acting. Making myself even more of a hero!

Finally, I allowed myself to take a glance at the illuminated dial of my watch. Fifteen minutes to go time.

I closed my eyes. I'd run through Joe the Hero a few more times. I pictured myself sneaking out of the—

Then a hand closed over my mouth.

(Not part of the movie.)

16.

THE TRUTH COMES OUT

The vibrator on my watch went off. Go time.

I opened my eyes and looked over at Joe. Make that Joe's bed. He wasn't in it.

I jerked my head toward Ken. He was there. Snoring away. Long, wet-sounding snores that would be very hard to fake.

I did a James bed check. Present.

Everyone in the bunk was present. Except Smiley.

You ever get one of those thoughts that are like a lightning bolt to your brain? Well, I got one of those babies the moment I saw Smiley's empty bed.

I knew Smiley had taken Joe. And I knew why.

Joe needed me for backup. I had to figure out where Smiley had taken him. I threw on clothes and shoes, grabbed the flashlight used for late-night latrine visits, and crept out of the cabin.

There were lots of tracks around the cabin. But I was able to spot fresh ones. Two sets. I followed them.

Even with the flashlight it was slow going. Then I heard a bunch of birds hit the air. That helped as much as any partial footprint or snapped twig.

An animal could have frightened those birds. But so could a couple of humans invading their territory. I hurried toward the sound.

And from there the trail was nice and clear. Two people had stood in this section of the woods. Not too long ago.

The tracks were heading toward the trail we took up the mountain. My gut told me I would find Joe up there. In the spot where Zack died.

I wanted to reach my brother immediately. The trail was wide enough to drive a jeep on. At least partway.

And I knew where I could find a jeep. I turned around and raced to Saunders's office. His jeep was parked outside.

I checked the ignition. Just in case this was my lucky night.

No. The keys weren't in it. Weren't in the glove compartment. Or in one of those little metal storage boxes you can hide under your car.

Not a problem. The jeep was old. Old and kind of cheap—which meant no armoring around the steering column.

I could hot-wire this baby and be gone in sixty seconds. All part of my ATAC training. Joe and I had gone undercover in a gang of teen car thieves on one of our missions.

There was a toolbox on the floor of the backseat. Nice. I grabbed a screwdriver and pried off the cover under the steering wheel, exposing a tangle of wires.

Beautiful sight. I touched the matching red wires together. The dash lit up. Another beautiful sight.

Now I just had to power up the starter motor. This time I mixed and matched the wires. I crossed the red wires with the brown lead. The engine kicked over. Ah, beautiful, beautiful sound.

Beautiful, beautiful sound that I hoped no one else had heard. . . . But if anyone had, they'd have to catch me to do anything about it.

I eased the Jeep away from the office. Then I floored it. I used the path that ran alongside the lake to take me to the base of the mountain. Then I ran the jeep straight up, until the trail got too narrow.

I put the jeep in park and jerked the wires apart. Then I leaped out and started to run. Man, the mountain was steep. I knew that from hiking it. But running—when you're running, the trail felt like it went straight up.

When I figured I was getting close to the spot where Zack had fallen to his death, I slowed down. I crept forward, staying close to the tree line, where I would be harder to see.

Smiley wasn't worried about anyone seeing him. I spotted him and Joe standing right in the spot where Saunders had asked us to observe a minute of silence for Zack.

I moved in closer, praying the shadows of the trees would keep me hidden. I was close enough to hear Smiley talking now.

I pulled a micro tape recorder out of my pocket and clicked it on. Joe and I were both hoping we'd get the killer saying something incriminating.

It's just that when we made the plan, we were thinking the killer was going to turn out to be Ken.

"Nobody will believe I'm a jumper," I heard Joe protest.

"Of course they will. Who would doubt that a loser like you would want to kill himself?" Smiley asked.

I wanted to hurl myself out of the shadows and

yank Joe away from the edge of the path. But I forced myself to wait.

"I would kill myself if I was as weak and pathetic as you. If I was going to keep my teammates from achieving victory," Smiley continued.

"You're crazy, Smiley," Joe said.

Nice. He got Smiley's name on the tape.

"No, nobody's gonna doubt for a second that you were a jumper," Smiley answered. "Especially because you decided to take the leap right where Zack bought it. Everyone will think you were feeling like a big loser. Just the way Zack was."

"Get your hands off me," Joe ordered. His voice was low and hard.

I'd heard enough. And I'd definitely seen enough. By the light of the stars and the half moon, I could see that Smiley had grabbed Joe by the shoulders.

I stepped out into the middle of the trail. "Yeah, take your hands off him."

Smiley turned his head toward me. But he kept his hands on Joe. "Neemy. What are you doing out here? This doesn't concern you."

"Oh, yes, it does," I answered. I wanted to move in closer. But I thought that might make Smiley try to push Joe off the edge of the path. I kept talking instead.

"Brian's one of my teammates. That makes him

my concern, right?" I asked. "And how do you think your father is going to feel about you killing one of the men on your team?" I was taking a chance—but I was ninety-nine percent sure I was right.

"His father?" Joe exclaimed.

Another voice echoed him.

Saunders stepped out onto the path. The guy was good. He'd clearly followed me after I stole the jeep. And I hadn't heard a sound out of him.

"I don't have a son," Saunders said.

Smiley's attention was totally on Saunders. Joe took that moment to twist out of Smiley's grasp and head over to me. Smiley hardly seemed to notice.

"You have quite a few genetic similarities," I said, mentally thanking my biology teacher. "You both have hairy knuckles. The code for that is located on gene one. You both have attached earlobes. That's a recessive trait. That means both of Smiley's parents had to have it."

"That doesn't prove anything," Saunders protested. His eyes were locked on Smiley.

"No, it doesn't. But it makes you think, doesn't it?" I asked. "You both have dimples. A dominant trait. You—"

"You were born in Montana. I remember that

from your file," Saunders said to Smiley.

"Montana, where you went to college," Joe jumped in. "You sure you didn't get friendly with someone there? You started college about twenty-five years ago. Maybe you met somebody in, say, your junior year. That would make the timing about right."

"What's your mother's name?" Saunders's voice came out hoarse. "Before she married Joe Smiley?"

"Her name was Annabeth Shapiro."

Saunders closed his eyes for a long moment. I was sure his brain had to be short-circuiting. "So you really are my son?"

Smiley nodded.

"Why didn't you tell me? And how did you find me?" Saunders asked.

The first question was like lighting the fuse to a bomb.

"I wanted to show you what I was made of first," Smiley exploded. "I wanted to prove that you could be proud of me. But the boys you put on my team were all such losers. Zack especially. And this one." Smiley jerked his chin toward Joe.

"Zack? You didn't. You couldn't have—" Saunders couldn't make himself actually say the words.

But Smiley answered anyway. "I eliminated him. For you. For the good of your reputation. I knew that's what you'd want. It's how you took care of the problem at Camp Character. You eliminated—"

"No!" Saunders cried. "You're talking about Samantha Previn. The canoeing accident. It was an accident. How can you have listened to my words and understood nothing?"

"This isn't the way you were supposed to find out." Smiley's voice turned high and whiny. "My team was going to win the race tomorrow. Because I was willing to eliminate the weakling." Again he nodded toward Joe.

Even in the starlight, I could see that Saunders's face had drained of blood.

"When we won, I was going to tell you," Smiley continued. "But now Neemy has ruined everything." He shot me a look filled with rage. Rage and despair. "You should be dead right now."

"Because you locked him in the boathouse and set it on fire," Joe said.

"You were furious that I'd made you look bad in front of your father, weren't you?" I asked. "He yelled at you because I told him that the guys on our team had given Brian a beating."

Saunders let out a cry that sounded like an animal with its foot caught in a trap. "This is true? It's all true?"

Smiley didn't deny it. He took a step toward his

father. Saunders backed away, as if Smiley was rabid.

Then Saunders pulled out his cell and dialed. A moment later he spoke into the phone. "This is Linc Saunders. I'm going to need the police over at my camp. I—"

He choked. Like he'd swallowed a bone. But he managed to go on. "I have Zack Maguire's killer."

Smiley sank down on the path. He looked like a puppet after the hand comes out of it.

I walked over to Saunders and handed him the micro recorder. "The police are going to want to hear what's on this."

The next day Joe and I were home. Being ATAC is surreal like that. You're on a mission. Hunting a murderer or something like that. Then it's over. And bam! Your biggest problem is getting your homework in on time. Or beating your little brother at basketball.

"I'm coming for you," Joe told me. "That's Joe Hardy. Not Mr. Spuddy. So watch out."

I dribbled my way toward the driveway hoop. Aunt Trudy came out of the house with some letters to mail. When she saw us playing, she dropped them.

And joined the game. She managed to snag the ball from me. She's surprisingly fast.

"Way to go, Aunt T," Joe yelled. She passed him the ball. He threw it at the hoop. Swish.

"I need teammates over here," I called. Mom and Dad were working in the garden. Well, Mom was working. Dad was reading the paper—over a break that had lasted all afternoon.

But even Dad couldn't resist a good b-ball game. He dropped the *Times* and took a position guarding Joe. I covered Aunt Trudy.

"Whose team am I on?" Mom asked as she stripped off her gardening gloves.

"Our team," Joe answered. "We need the handicap."

"Very funny," Mom muttered. She took a position on the tiny court.

Actually Mom's not a bad player. Maybe she's where Joe and I got our b-ball skill. Or maybe we got it from Dad.

Aunt Trudy let out a teenage girl kind of squeal as she made a basket. The ball sailed through the net, without touching the rim.

"Score!" Joe called. "Nice teamwork, Aunt T." He winked at me.

The talent was *definitely* in the gene pool someplace.

CLUE IN TO THE CLASSIC MYSTERIES OF THE HARDY BOYS®
FROM GROSSET & DUNLAP

$6.99 ($9.99 CAN) each

AVAILABLE AT YOUR LOCAL BOOKSTORE OR LIBRARY

Grosset & Dunlap • A division of Penguin Young Readers Group
A member of Penguin Group (USA), Inc. • A Pearson Company
www.penguin.com/youngreaders

THE HARDY BOYS is a trademark of Simon & Schuster, Inc., registered in the United States Patent and Trademark Office.